CAPTURED AT LAST?

Holt cocked back the hammer of his Colt and aimed it at Joe's chest. "All right, Moss. Keep your hands up in the air and walk straight toward me."

Joe knew that the man would not hesitate to kill him if he made the slightest wrong move. "You got me cold," he said. "Just go easy on that trigger."

"That's close enough," Holt said when Joe was less than ten feet from him. "Did you really think that we'd give up the chase?"

"Nope," Joe said. "I always knew that sooner or later it would come down to this. To just you and me."

Holt's face was red, wet with perspiration, and plastered with sand where it had struck the dunes when his horse was shot. "If you weren't worth so much more to Mr. Peabody alive than dead, I'd blow a hole in you right now. I'd gut-shoot you so you'd flop down in this sand and die screaming. And maybe I would even scalp you before your last breath so you could taste a little of your own Injun medicine."

Joe said nothing, but his mind was exploring every possible way he could kill this man before being tied hand and foot and taken to be hanged on the Comstock Lode . . .

Titles by Gary Franklin

MAN OF HONOR
THE MOTHER LODE
BLOOD AT BEAR LAKE
COMSTOCK CROSS FIRE

COMSTOCK CROSS FIRE

A Man of Honor Novel

GARY FRANKLIN

BERKLEY BOOKS, NEW YORK

THE BERKLEY PUBLISHING GROUP
Published by the Penguin Group
Penguin Group (USA) Inc.
375 Hudson Street, New York, New York 10014, USA
Penguin Group (Canada), 90 Eglinton Avenue East, Suite 700, Toronto, Ontario M4P 2Y3, Canada
(a division of Pearson Penguin Canada Inc.)
Penguin Books Ltd., 80 Strand, London WC2R 0RL, England
Penguin Group Ireland, 25 St. Stephen's Green, Dublin 2, Ireland (a division of Penguin Books Ltd.)
Penguin Group (Australia), 250 Camberwell Road, Camberwell, Victoria 3124, Australia
(a division of Pearson Australia Group Pty. Ltd.)
Penguin Books India Pvt. Ltd., 11 Community Centre, Panchsheel Park, New Delhi—110 017, India
Penguin Group (NZ), 67 Apollo Drive, Rosedale, North Shore 0632, New Zealand
(a division of Pearson New Zealand Ltd.)
Penguin Books (South Africa) (Pty.) Ltd., 24 Sturdee Avenue, Rosebank, Johannesburg 2196,
South Africa

Penguin Books Ltd., Registered Offices: 80 Strand, London WC2R 0RL, England

This is a work of fiction. Names, characters, places, and incidents either are the product of the author's imagination or are used fictitiously, and any resemblance to actual persons, living or dead, business establishments, events, or locales is entirely coincidental.

COMSTOCK CROSS FIRE

A Berkley Book / published by arrangement with the author

PRINTING HISTORY
Berkley edition / December 2008

Copyright © 2008 by Gary McCarthy.
Cover illustration by Bill Angresano.
Cover design by Steven Ferlauto.

ISBN: 978-0-425-22487-8

BERKLEY®
Berkley Books are published by The Berkley Publishing Group,
a division of Penguin Group (USA) Inc.,
375 Hudson Street, New York, New York 10014.
BERKLEY® is a registered trademark of Penguin Group (USA) Inc.
The "B" design is a trademark belonging to Penguin Group (USA) Inc.

PRINTED IN THE UNITED STATES OF AMERICA

10 9 8 7 6 5 4 3 2 1

✤ 1 ✤

AFTER REMOVING HER chains and shackles, Joe Moss held his wife, Fiona, as if she were as fragile as a piece of ancient Indian pottery. Beside him lay two unconscious bounty hunters who had been holding her hostage; Joe figured to kill and then scalp them just as soon as he got his woman settled down a mite.

"Fiona," he whispered as she sobbed uncontrollably in his arms. "Please don't be cryin' so hard. What is done is done and what is to come will work out fine."

"They *raped* me!" she sobbed, twisting away to glare at the two filthy men that Joe had knocked unconscious with his tomahawk. "They made me do disgusting things that . . . oh, Joe, I was prayin' to die. I . . ."

He crushed her in his arms. "Fiona, what is done is done, but there's a lot more that we're gonna have to face in the days to come."

A long, ragged sigh rattled from Fiona's throat, and he smoothed her dirty red hair, remembering how it used to shine in the sunlight when he'd first met and fallen in love with her years ago on the California-bound wagon train. He'd spent so long trying to find her and their daughter, but every turn of the road seemed to have been the wrong one, and now . . . at last . . . they were together again. Both hurt badly, both scarred by others, yet still alive and still in love.

"Where are we?" she whispered, her body seeming so slight and frail against his powerful frame. "They blind-folded me. Kept me that way for what seemed like forever. I don't even know where I am, Joe! I don't know who I am anymore! I just . . ."

Fiona broke down in hysterics and her knees buckled. Joe Moss picked her up and stepped over the two unconscious men who lay bleeding from their severe head wounds. He started to carry his wife into the dugout, then caught the scent of what was inside and changed direction, moving toward a mound of hay out by the corral. Easing Fiona down on the fresh-mowed hay, he found a rag and then dipped it into the horse-watering trough. "You're all dirty now," he explained as he gently washed Fiona's bruised and tear-stained face, "but I'm going to make you clean again."

Fiona looked up at him and her eyes were so filled with sorrow that, for the briefest of moments, Joe Moss felt utter despair. He wondered if his wife's mind and spirit might finally have been broken beyond repair. Her next words only reinforced that dread.

"Joe, you can't wash away what those . . . those animals did to me these last few weeks. Not if you scrubbed me with lye soap for a hundred years, because nothing will *ever* wash away the hideous things that they did to me!"

Joe desperately tried to find the right words to make her feel that someday she would feel clean and wholesome again, but the words just wouldn't come out. He was a mountain man, a loner, and not one gifted with words; he never had been and never would be. But staring into her green eyes and seeing all that pain told Joe that he had to try to help his woman, so he said, "Those two that used you so bad are waiting for a man named Ransom Holt."

"I know. He's all that they talked about. They told me that Holt would chop off my head and put it in a wooden keg filled with spirits and then they'd . . ."

Fiona's entire body convulsed with horror. She covered her face and sobbed.

"Easy, easy" Joe crooned, feeling his throat well up so bad that he could hardly swallow. "It ain't your head that's gonna get chopped off and pickled in any barrel. It'll be the head of Ransom Holt. He's on his way here, paid by a rich Comstock Lode mine owner. He means t' bring back your pretty head pickled in a barrel. Only Mr. Peabody ain't goin' to get your head. It'll be Ransom's head, by gawd."

Joe got Fiona settled down a little, and then he removed her dirty dress and laid her out naked to be washed. He remembered how her body had looked when he'd first tasted it on the Oregon Trail five years ago. Her body had been lush, smooth, virginal, and as white as freshly fallen snow. Now it was skin and bone, scarred and covered with bruises and festering. He saw bite marks and signs that she had been whipped. The sight of what had been done to his wife filled Joe with a fury he'd never known before. It was all that he could do not to grab his tomahawk and charge over to the two bounty hunters and hack them into bloody pieces.

Instead, Joe shook himself and got control. He managed to croak, "Fiona, is there any soap in that dugout?"

"No." Her hand flew up and grabbed his collar and she cried, "Joe, can't you understand that soap won't wash away my sin? Nothing can wash away . . ."

He placed his forefinger on her lips and silenced that talk. "Fiona, you're my wife and we got a child to think of back in Virginia City. We got four-year-old Jessica Moss that's waitin' in that cold church convent for us to come back and claim her. We got t' be strong for our daughter or . . . or we'll never see her again. Neither of us."

Fiona closed her eyes, and she seemed to gather some deep and hidden strength. "Yes, you're right. We have Jessica. But—"

"But what?" Joe asked, not wanting to know.

Fiona opened her eyes and stared up at Joe. "Bad luck seems to be our lot. Everything we do and everything we touch seems to go rotten or wrong. Maybe . . . maybe we should just let our daughter be raised by those sweet nuns at St. Mary's! Maybe if she becomes one of them someday, she'll never, ever have to suffer what we've suffered!"

Joe's voice hardened and he shook his shaggy head like a wolf tearing at frozen flesh. "Don't say that! Don't *ever* say that again, Fiona. I'm Jessica's father and you're her mother. She *needs* us. We'll get through all this and come out okay. And we'll raise Jessica, and maybe even more, to be strong and good."

Fiona's chin dipped. "Can we do that, Joe? Can we ever get past all the evil that's come upon us and come to be good and strong? Become the kind of mother and father that Jessica deserves and should have?"

"Hell, yes, we can! We're already strong. And as for the bad luck, well, it changes." He looked away and his voice fell to a hush. "At least, sometimes it can."

"But can it for *us*?" There was urgency in her voice that went beyond desperation.

Joe didn't know the answer to her question, but Fiona desperately needed reassurance, so he squared his broad shoulders and declared, "Our luck already has changed t' the good, Fiona. If it hadn't, you wouldn't be alive and neither would I."

"But Ransom Holt is coming and even if you kill him, Mr.

Peabody will send someone to take his place. Mr. Peabody will always be sending someone to kill us. To chop off our heads and—"

"Don't!" Joe said, clenching his big fists and raising them high overhead. "Don't say any of that anymore. I'm gonna kill Ransom when he comes, and then I'm gonna take *his* head, pickle and pack it across the desert to Peabody. When I face that rich man in Virginia City, I'm gonna tear Ransom Holt's pickled head out by the hair and I'm gonna beat Peabody to death with that severed head!"

Joe's fury was so terrible that Fiona actually shrank back in shock and fear. Seeing the effect his words had had on his wife, Joe unclenched his fists and lowered his arms. "I'm sorry, darlin'. Didn't mean to scare you any more than you've already been scared. But I got a powerful need to kill and scalp those two that was holding you hostage while rapin' and nearly starvin' you to death. I'm gonna do it when they wake up so they can feel the blade of my 'hawk slicin' through their skins. I'm gonna send them both to Hell screamin' like the hounds of Hell are after them. And then I'm gonna wait for Ransom Holt and do the same thing to him."

Fiona sat up and her lips moved without words until she got control of her voice. "Joe, I want you to kill those two horrible men. You can even slosh a bucket of water on 'em so they know they're going to die before you kill 'em. But then let's just pack up and leave with the horses. Let's just get away from this evilness and never look back or talk about what was done to me here or what was done to them either."

Joe blinked. "You mean you want us t' just run away?"

"Yes! I've seen so much blood and death that I want to leave it all behind! Let's go to Virginia City and claim our daughter and then . . . please . . . let's find a place where Ransom Holt or whoever else that Garrison Peabody sends will never, ever find us."

Joe stood up and shook his head. "I'm sorry, Fiona, but there ain't no such a place. Sooner or later, Peabody or Holt or someone we never even heard of but who was out to get paid t' kill us would come. It might take 'em a year, maybe ten. Maybe even fifty, when we're old and gray . . . but by gawd come they would! Rich people like the Peabody family won't ever let this go until it's all finished. And that means I gotta kill the last Peabody before he sends someone that finally kills us."

Fiona had listened, but she wasn't really listening. "Joe," she begged, "you know the West. You've trapped beaver, drove freight wagons, ridden, walked, or ran the rivers across every square mile of this big, wide frontier. I can't believe that you don't know places where Peabody and his people would never find us."

"I have done all that, Fiona, but—"

"Please, think about us hiding in one of those secret places you camped in long ago while trapping beaver! Think about it for me. For Jessica. For yourself, too, Joe. For us as a family, please try and think of where we could go and spend the rest of our lives without being found."

Joe expelled a deep breath. He looked up at the Wasatch Mountains, some of the boldest and emptiest he'd ever trapped or hunted in. Then he looked down at his poor, abused wife and raised her naked to her feet. "Look all around you, woman."

Joe swept an arm out in a wide, all-encompassing circle. "Fiona, what do you see?"

"I see mountains. Trees. Sky and a lake way off there. A beautiful lake. Where am I?"

"This is Bear Lake in the Utah Territory. Brigham Young's got a city he's building off to the west a ways, and there's a great salt lake that won't let a man drown even if he's dead drunk. And these mountains . . . well, darlin', I know these mountains like the back of my hand. I used to trap in these mountains and we had our rendezvous here at Bear Lake. There are places in these mountains so wild that even the Indians are scarce t' find."

Her face took on an expression of hope. "Then after we take Jessica back from the Catholic nuns, we could come back to these parts and hide forever up in these mountains. Joe, I swear that we could build us a nice log cabin. Put in a truck garden and raise some livestock. You could—"

"Shhh," he ordered, his voice soft and sad.

Her mouth was open and she found it hard to stop the torrent of dreams she was spinning out for them. "But, Joe, we—"

"We'd live every day wonderin' if someone was comin' to find us. And, darlin', sooner or later, if the bounty was big enough, someone *would* find us. And then maybe they'd kill not only the two of us, but also our little girl and any other babies we might have borned." Joe squeezed her hands. "Fiona, is that what you want to happen?"

"Of course not! But . . . but how could you be so sure that we'd be found? These mountains, why, they seem to go on forever!"

"They don't," Joe said, an even deeper sadness in his words. "I once thought they did . . . but I learned they just don't. And, darlin', there are men like myself who have trapped and hunted all through these mountains. And, if offered a fortune by Peabody, they'd come and find us. They'd be hard, hungry men. Men like me who had seen their way of life taken from them and who hadn't found a path or a place for themselves since. And . . . and they'd think about that Peabody bounty and what it might do for 'em and they'd be willin' t' kill or be killed for another chance at what they'd lost."

He could tell that she didn't want to believe him. "Would they, Joe? Would they really?"

"Yep. I would were I them."

"No!" she cried. "You wouldn't sneak up on a man and his wife and child and kill them for money!"

"I killed women before," he admitted. "I've killed for a lot less money than Peabody would be offerin'."

Fiona quickly looked away, and when Joe tried to reach out and turn her around to face him, she pulled out of his reach.

"Fiona," he said, seeing how her whole thin body was trembling. "I *have* killed women. But none of 'em for money. An' I killed a couple of murderin' whores once down in Santa Fe. But I swear that I ain't killed anyone for money since I've knowed you. I swear it."

She turned to face him, and she searched every inch of his scarred face looking for truth. Finally, she said, "I believe you."

"And you also need t' trust me," he told her. "Trust me to know what I'm doin' is the right thing . . . the only thing . . . that can save us."

After a long moment, Fiona dipped her chin. "So how are you going to kill Ransom Holt when he comes here to collect my head?"

"I don't rightly know yet," Joe admitted. "Holt has my description, sure as anything, just like I know what he looks like. But he's never laid eyes on me and that's the advantage."

"What if he brings men with him? What if he's got men to help him?"

"Then I'll kill them, too," Joe vowed. "I'll just kill all them dirty sonsabitches."

"You're that sure you can do it?"

"I am," Joe Moss vowed. "As God is my witness and you are my love and my life, I will kill whoever comes—right to the very last man."

Fiona shivered as a breeze touched her thin, bruised body. She looked over at the two unconscious bounty hunters that Joe had laid low, and then she said, "All right, Joe. Kill those two now and then we'll kill Ransom Holt and anyone else who comes for my head."

Joe drew out his tomahawk and spotted a rusty tin water bucket. He grabbed the bucket and filled it from the trough, saying, "Fiona, maybe you ought t' go inside that dugout for a few minutes and get whatever is worth takin'. I'll do what needs doin' out here."

"Are you going to wake them up and kill them slow?"

"Yep. That's 'xactly what I have in mind."

"Then I need to watch."

Joe was a hard man and not surprised by much of anything, but when his sweet Fiona uttered those words, he was shaken to the marrow of his bones. "You want t' watch them die screaming and being scalped? It'll be a slow, bloody thing."

"They did slow, bloody things to me in that dugout," Fiona said, her eyes hard and fierce. "An eye for an eye, a tooth for a tooth, sayeth the Lord."

"And so it will be," Joe replied as he drew his tomahawk, threw back his head, and sang out to the sky a terrible, primal scream.

The Indians called him Man Killer, and today he would add fresh scalps to his belt as God and Fiona would witness.

"WHAT'S THIS SONOFABITCH'S name?" Joe asked, ready to dump the pail of water on the bounty hunter's bleeding head.

"That's the one in charge," Fiona said, pointing a shaky finger at the unconscious man. "His name is Jedediah Charles. The other one is named Ike. I never heard his last name."

Joe raised the bucket and emptied its cold contents on Jedediah Charles. Both of the unconscious bounty hunters had taken hard whacks across the skull from the flat of Joe's tomahawk, but he'd hit Jedediah the hardest. Now Joe was wondering if this one could be revived or if his skull had been fatally crushed.

Jedediah stirred and moaned. "He's alive," Joe announced, going for another pail of water. "But he's in bad shape."

"Maybe you should just let him die," Fiona hedged, suddenly feeling a twinge of guilt despite the terrible outrages that had been committed against her body by the pair.

"Too easy," Joe said, bringing back the second pail and sloshing it in the man's face, bringing him to full wakefulness.

Jedediah coughed and sat up, his eyes still dazed. He blinked and sputtered; then his eyes regained their focus and he stared at Joe Moss, who was drawing his tomahawk from his belt sash. At the sight of Joe and the bloodstained tomahawk, Jedediah became fully alert. He tried to scoot backward in the mud, but Joe jumped forward, grabbed him by the shirtfront, and then used his tomahawk to slice off one of the struggling man's ears.

Jedediah screamed and clapped his hands against the side of his head, trying to staunch all the blood pouring through his fingers. Joe had a remedy for that. He dropped his tomahawk, drew his bowie knife, and cut off all the man's fingers on both hands, leaving only his quivering thumbs.

"Ahhh!" the man screamed at the top of his lungs. "Oh, my gawd, you're killin' me!"

"How's it feeling?" Joe asked as the bounty hunter howled. "You liked rapin' and starvin' my poor wife, did you?"

"No!" Jedediah bawled. "I'm sorry! Honest to God I'm sorry! Don't do this to me!"

"You're sorry?" Joe asked, his voice as dry and brittle as broken glass. "Why, Jedediah, you haven't began t' learn what sorry really is."

Joe grabbed the man's long, greasy hair, and with practiced ease he cut a plate-sized piece of scalp. Jedediah howled even louder when Joe dangled the man's scalp before his bulging eyes. "How's it look to ya now, Jed? Take a good, long, and last look, you sorry, stinking piece of dog shit!"

"Joe, I can't stand this!" Fiona cried in protest. "Just put him out of his misery."

"He'll have to do that for his own damn self," Joe said, his own blood hot with revenge as he went to get another pail of water and rouse the second bounty hunter for slaughter.

About a mile to the south and behind a rocky bluff, Ransom Holt reined in his horse and raised a hand for silence. "Someone is dying," he said, more to himself than to the two hired killers who rode at his side. "Dying hard, too."

"Do you think that Jedediah Charles is killin' the Moss woman right now?" one of the men asked.

"No," Holt decided. "I've heard women screaming in childbirth and none ever sounded like that. It's a man that's dyin'."

"Maybe one of them is killing the other over the Moss woman."

"Maybe," Holt conceded. "It could also be Indians having their blood sport. But I'm thinking that Joe Moss somehow found the dugout and his wife. If that happened, then I believe that he is taking his bloody revenge on Jedediah and his partner."

The two hired killers exchanged glances, and the one named Dalton said, "If that's the case, we can kill Moss and get *two* rewards from Mr. Peabody. One for Joe and one for his wife."

"Wait a minute," said the one named Eli. "Didn't Mr. Peabody change his mind and say he wanted them both brought back alive so that they could be hanged in Virginia City?"

"That's right," Holt agreed, dragging out his six-gun and making sure it was ready. "Mr. Peabody has a hangman and two nooses waiting, the *choking* kind of nooses. He wants to see Moss and his woman strangle to death on a tree limb. So, boys, this could be our lucky day because those two are worth more to Peabody alive than dead."

One of the hired killers pulled a double-barreled shotgun out of its scabbard, saying, "Moss won't be captured without a hard fight. Everything we've heard about the man is bad, and the Indians we talked to don't call him Man Killer for nothin'."

Ransom Holt snorted with derision. "Moss is just an old trapper well past his prime. He's dangerous, sure. But he's no match for the three of us. Now, is he?"

"Hell, no!" the brothers replied in unison.

Holt studied the men. "Glad to hear you boys say that. If we can take Moss and his woman alive, you'll be paid double what you were already promised."

"In Comstock gold," Dalton said, patting the butt of a buffalo rifle that he could use to shoot down a man with deadly accuracy from a half mile's distance.

"Yeah," Holt agreed. "In Comstock gold."

Eli and Dalton were brothers known for their random and constant viciousness. They were of average size physically, but there was a deadly aura about both men that gave even Ransom Holt cause for concern. If Eli and Dalton even suspected that they could deliver Moss and his wife to Peabody and collect all the bounty money, Holt knew he was likely to be back-shot between the Utah Territory and Nevada.

Holt sat a moment longer, listening to the horrible screams of someone who was obviously being tortured to death by an expert. Ransom Holt was a very, very big and powerful man. He knew that Joe Moss was also said to stand tall . . . a couple inches over six feet . . . but Holt was six feet five and he was younger, heavier, and stronger than Joe Moss. He had almost been hoping to kill Moss with his bare hands, but after hearing of all the dead men that Moss had scalped, Holt decided that it would be foolish to take a chance.

Let Eli and Dalton earn their pay here and now. Let them take Moss down, and then let them help me get the two captives up to the base of the Comstock Lode, before I kill the brothers and take Peabody's money all for myself. And yes, it would all be in Comstock gold.

"How do you want to handle this?" Dalton asked, wiping his face with the back of his dirty sleeve.

Holt gave the question some serious thought before he answered. "I've been dogging Joe Moss and his whore a long, long time. He's murdered enough of my informants to have gotten my description. He'll recognize me by my size the second he lays eyes on me from any distance. So here's what we'll do, boys."

Ransom Holt quickly outlined a simple, but what he believed would be an effective, plan to take Moss alive.

"That's it," he said. "Eli and I will circle around behind that dugout. Give us an hour, Dalton. Then you ride straight in like you were ignorant and prove to us how accurate you really are with that buffalo gun. Shoot Moss, but don't you dare kill the man, because we've already agreed that would cost us a lot of gold."

Dalton nodded with understanding, yet he had a question. "But won't Moss figure I heard the screams and came to interfere?"

"That's why we'll wait an hour before we close in behind Moss . . . or whoever else is doing the killing and torturing."

Dalton licked his lips because he was getting more and more nervous. "I don't like to be separated from my brother, Mr. Holt. Maybe—"

"*Maybe,*" Holt spat, "you should just do what I've ordered! Or else maybe you and Eli should turn those horses around and ride out with your damned empty pockets and I'll take all that reward money from Peabody!"

The two brothers exchanged glances, and they could read each other's minds.

"All right," Eli, who was the older and the leader of the brothers, finally decided out loud. "We'll do it exactly as you say, Mr. Holt. But I want to have Moss in my gun sights before my brother rides up to that dugout. If it's really Joe Moss that's doin' the torturin', he's a crack shot and he'd not hesitate to shoot my brother right out of his saddle."

"Fair enough," Holt agreed.

The brothers nodded to each other in mutual acceptance.

"Then let's get to it," Holt said, feeling his heart begin to pound. He'd been searching for Joe Moss and his woman for long, hard months, and now he was just about to have them both.

"Gawd, that's a different one screaming now," Eli said, cocking an ear to the north. "Screaming even louder than the first did."

"My money says that we're about to meet Joe Moss at last," Holt replied, picking up his reins. "I just hope that his woman is still alive so that we can take them both back to Virginia City."

"If she ain't, we can still take her head back, can't we?"

"Sure," Holt said. "Peabody wouldn't be satisfied without her head. Just hope that the pickling doesn't wrinkle her face up so much that she is beyond recognition by the time we reach the Comstock Lode."

"Or bleach out her red hair," Eli mused with morbid curiosity. "I've a notion that could happen to red hair."

Holt frowned because he hadn't taken that into consideration. "Maybe if the woman is dead, we can cut off her head and pack it in salt. Might hold up better in the heat across the desert."

"Might," Dalton said. "Salt would crust up the blood and hair, but it might not change the red color."

"Might not at that," Eli agreed with an eager smile.

"Let's ride," Holt ordered. "Dalton, you got a watch so you'll know when the hour is up?"

"Yeah," the man said, pulling out a cheap pocket watch and consulting its face. "Stole it off a drunk whose throat I cut when he was passed out in Laramie."

"It's now two-ten? Right?" Holt asked, consulting his fine gold pocket watch.

"Close enough," Dalton said, grinning. "Eli, you better have him in your sights by ten minutes after three."

"Oh, I will," Eli promised as he rode away following Ransom Holt.

✛ 3 ✛

"ARE THEY BOTH dead, Joe?"

"Yeah, well, almost." Joe held up their bloody scalps. "These will go with the others I've taken."

Fiona had come out of the dugout carrying a feed sack filled with salt pork and a few other things of little value. She had also found what a poor Indian woman might consider to be a dress. Now she stopped and stared at the two bodies. "Joe, Ike is still breathing."

"He's knockin' on Hell's gates," Joe said. "But he just don't have the strength left to knock very loud."

Fiona forced herself to look at the two still figures. "You can't just leave them here like that!"

"I'll be damned if I'll bury the likes of 'em," Joe vowed.

"But . . ."

Joe's voice hardened. "After what they did to you, why should you care?"

"I don't know," she admitted. "But I don't want to just leave them out here to rot or be eaten by animals. And . . ."

She couldn't finish.

"And what?" Joe asked.

"And I can't abide you carrying their scalps."

Joe frowned. "Fiona, I carry all the scalps of them that did me wrong and I kilt to settle the score."

"Please," she whispered. "Just . . . just leave them here. Leave all your scalps here."

Joe's pride was offended, but when he looked at his poor wife and realized how much suffering and torment she'd endured, he could not refuse her simple request.

"All right," he agreed. "I'll drag these dyin' bastards into that dugout and toss in their scalps along with the others I got. Then we'll fire it all up and send 'em on their merry way to Hell."

"Thank you," Fiona said with obvious relief. "We're going to get our daughter back from the nuns. Our darling little Jessica. We can't have her ever knowing what took place here. Do you understand me, Joe?"

"You mean you don't want her to know about this pair and how I kilt, then scalped 'em?"

"That and what they did to me. It's our secret cross to bear."

"I ain't bearin' no cross of no kind," Joe argued. "I kilt these two and I wish I could have kilt 'em over and over 'cause of what they done to you, Fiona. I can't change the way I feel about that."

"I know. But this is something I want to put behind us."

"Sure," he said with some confusion. "We'll . . ." Joe's words froze in his throat. "Man on horseback comin' this way."

Fiona shrank back toward the dugout. "Oh, Joe, don't let them get me again! Please."

Joe reached for his Henry rifle and levered a shell. "Ain't nobody ever going to hurt you again," he promised, watching the horseman trot steadily toward them and noting that the horseman carried a big rifle in his hands.

"Is it Ransom Holt?" Fiona cried, her lips trembling. "Is it Ransom Holt comin' to chop off my head?"

"It ain't Holt," Joe assured her. "I been told Holt is a big, big man. This 'un is average-sized. It ain't Holt and he ain't goin' to hurt either one of us. If anyone else is gonna die this day, it'll be this man a-comin'."

"Joe, he's dismounting!"

Joe's eyes narrowed and he watched the man tie his horse to a tree next to a fallen log. To Joe's amazement the stranger actually waved, and then sat down behind the tree and laid his big rifle across the log.

"Fiona, get inside the dugout!" Joe shouted, grabbing and shoving her toward the hole in the hillside.

Fiona threw herself at the dugout's entrance, and disappeared just as the big buffalo rifle boomed.

A second later, Joe heard a faint whistle, then the sound of the heavy-caliber slug as it struck the side of the dugout, missing him by less than a foot. He saw the lone rifleman begin to reload what Joe knew from its bark was a .52-caliber breech-loading Sharps. Joe knew that the man was good and that he wouldn't miss a second time, but he also knew that the killer would have to reload the Sharps and that would take him about twenty precious seconds.

"Goddamn you!" Joe bellowed, bursting into a hard run toward the man behind the log. If he was fast enough, he might be able to get to the rifleman before he could reload. There really wasn't much cover between him and the man with the buffalo rifle, but Joe was slender and fast. He'd get him or he'd shoot him dead at close range.

Either way, the stranger was as good as scalped.

Joe was halfway to the rifleman and had his own Henry rifle up and ready to fire when he heard a shrill scream from behind. His head whipped around and he saw Ransom Holt and another man with a shotgun burst out into the open. Fiona was nowhere in sight. Holt jumped into the dugout and the man with the shotgun stood guard outside.

Joe skidded to a halt and turned to shoot the man with the shotgun even as Fiona's screams reached his ears from inside the dugout.

"Fiona!" he shouted. "I'm comin'!"

In his panic, Joe fired on the run, which was dumb, and he missed. He grabbed the revolver at his side and raised it, but then something like the kick of a mule hit him in the back and he went down. The last thing he heard was Fiona's final scream and then he lost consciousness, shot in the back by the buffalo rifle.

"Is he alive?" a gravelly voice asked.

"Yeah. He's hit bad, but I shot to wound, not kill, 'cause I remembered you sayin' Mr. Peabody would pay us more if they was alive."

"Good damn thing that you remembered, Dalton. Get the woman to bandage her man up so he don't bleed out on us."

Dalton went into the dugout and returned dragging Fiona by one arm. "You struck her pretty hard with the butt of your pistol, Mr. Holt. Maybe scrambled her brains."

"That doesn't matter," Ransom Holt snapped. "Mr. Peabody doesn't care if she's addled or not. All he said was that he wanted her back alive so that he could hang her in Virginia City along with Joe Moss."

"Moss might not make it either."

"He'll make it," Holt vowed. "He's the toughest son-ofabitch I've ever heard of and he just won't die."

"My Sharps put a hole right through his shoulder and maybe his lung."

"If he's lung-shot, then I guess he will die," Holt said. "And it'll cost you plenty."

The rifleman's face flushed with anger. "He was runnin' when I brought him down. I had to shoot him on the run, Mr. Holt! And I had to make sure I didn't miss or he'd have kilt you and my brother both!"

Ransom Holt knew this was probably true. "I guess you're right, but we got to try and stop that bleeding and keep Moss alive until we can deliver him to Peabody."

"Maybe the woman can figure a way to save her man," Dalton offered.

Holt swore in frustration. "Enough of this damned jabbering! Get that pail and fill it with water. Wake her up and we'll see if that little redheaded slut is any good at doctoring."

Moments later, Fiona burst into awareness fighting for air and feeling as if she were being drowned. When she tried to climb to her feet, strong hands grabbed her by the arms, pulled her erect, and then one of the biggest men she had ever seen in her life snarled in her face, "Your husband was shot high in the back by a Sharps rifle. He's bleeding bad. You'd better stop that bleeding or he's going to die. Live or die, it's up to you, Mrs. Moss."

Fiona knew that this was Ransom Holt who had her by the arms. She looked into his black eyes and also knew that he was a man without pity or even a soul. He was only half human, if that much.

Then she tore her eyes away from Holt's cruel face and saw Joe lying facedown in the dirt with a large wound in the upper part of his left shoulder. Fiona tore free from Holt and collapsed at her husband's side.

"Joe! Joe!"

"He's unconscious, you stupid whore!" Dalton growled. "You better plug up that bullet hole on both sides or he's a goner."

Though nearly out of her mind with fear, Fiona understood that the man who had shot her husband was correct. Joe was bleeding to death and no one except herself was going to raise a hand to save him.

All three men stood around her staring downward at Joe. Finally, Ransom Holt hissed, "Get her some rags to plug up that shoulder. Get her whatever she needs to save that scalpin' sonofabitch's life. Remember, if Joe Moss lives, we all have extra bounty gold in our pockets. Peabody wants them both to hang side by side kickin' and gaggin' in Virginia City."

Holt chuckled, then added, "And Peabody is even gonna charge admission to watch these two hang. Gonna charge five dollars a head and he expects there to be *thousands* of Comstock Lode miners cheerin' and hollerin' as Moss and his woman dance and strangle."

The two brothers hurried toward the dugout, and Fiona realized what Holt had just said and she stored this valuable piece of information away. Ransom Holt and these men had been ordered to bring her and Joe back to Virginia City alive.

That being the case, there was now just the faintest glimmer of hope. If she and Joe had to be taken all the way to the Comstock Lode, there would be time for Joe to heal. Time for them to figure out some way to escape . . . or even to kill these three rabid animals.

But then Fiona also realized that there would also be plenty of time and opportunity for these men to use her like a bitch in heat. And when she thought of that possibility, after all the humiliation she had already suffered at the hands of the scalped pair, Fiona nearly lost what was left of her mind.

Had it not been for her dear Joe bleeding so bad, Fiona would have grabbed the bowie knife from his sash and in one quick, final motion of defiance and liberation, she would have slit her own throat and died beside her poor mountain man.

Holt broke into her terrible thoughts. "Do you think he's going to make it?"

"I don't know," Fiona replied. "If he had to be shot, why didn't you tell your ambusher to shoot my husband in the legs?"

Holt scratched at his beard. "It was a long-distance shot and a running man's legs are too hard a target."

"Well," Fiona said, "I can stop the bleeding, but my husband is going to need a doctor and some mending time in bed."

"Not a chance," Holt snapped.

"If Joe doesn't get a doctor and some time to rest and heal, then he'll die for certain."

"Too bad," Holt said without a shred of real sympathy.

"Too bad for *you*," Fiona managed to summon up the courage to say. "Because from what I've just overheard, if Joe dies, it is going to cost you a lot of Peabody's blood money."

Holt was impressed by her insight. "You got a skinny body, but your hearing and reasoning is still good."

Fiona rested her head against Joe's back and listened. "The slug didn't hit him in the lung," she said more to herself than to Holt. "That means that he's still got a fighting chance."

"Oh," Holt said, "he'll survive. I've heard enough stories about Joe Moss to know that he's almost impossible to kill."

"He is," Fiona said with as much pride as she could muster. "And someday you'll find that out and it will be the last lesson you'll ever learn."

Holt threw back his head and laughed at the sky. "I'll give this much to you, Fiona Moss. You've got sand. Yep, you've got sand in your craw. So how did Jedediah and Ike treat you in the dugout while I was coming?"

She twisted her head and gazed up at the huge man. "They treated me like a dog. But I'm alive now and they're dead. So what does that tell *you*?"

He laughed again. "It tells me that I don't have to pay Jedediah and Ike a thing and that means more money in my own pocket, which suits me just fine."

"Are you going to even bury them?"

"Hell, no!"

"Then at least drag them into that filthy dugout and set them on fire so the animals don't eat their bodies," Fiona said. "You owe them that much."

Holt hooked his big thumbs into his cartridge belt and frowned. "Why should you care what happens to their bodies after they treated you like a dog?"

"Because I'm a human being, Mr. Holt."

"Yeah, so I've heard. And you murdered Chester J. Peabody one night at your little house in Virginia City."

"I didn't murder him! Someone else did!"

"Yeah, well, then, why did they find Chester dead in your house with a knife still sticking out of his back and blood all over you *and* your front room?"

"Because he was murdered outside my house and I dragged him inside to see if I could save his life. But Mr. Peabody was already dead."

Holt shook his head in obvious disbelief. "I don't buy a word of that," he told her. "And it doesn't matter anymore. Your husband killed two more of the brothers down by St. Mary's Church when you got on your horse and ran out on him."

"He made me go," Fiona said quietly with fresh tears coming to her eyes. "I didn't want to leave Joe, but he said that if he was killed, I needed to stay alive for our daughter."

"How very, very touching," Holt said, voice dripping

with sarcasm. "Well, you can tell your sad story to Garrison Peabody. He's the only one left standing and now he's the sole owner of the Shamrock Mine in Gold Hill. That means he's as rich as a king, and he won't ever stop until he sees you and Joe swinging side by side at the end of a strangler's noose."

Fiona shivered. "If I could talk to Garrison Peabody, maybe I could convince him that I really didn't kill his brother that night."

"And what damned good would that do?" Holt asked with amusement. "Because even if you somehow did convince Peabody that you didn't murder his oldest brother that night on the Comstock, how would you explain that your husband shot his other two brothers and also blew up his mine with dynamite?"

She looked away, thinking hard, and the best she could say was, "Joe was only acting in self-defense."

"Ha! I want to be there when you tell Peabody *that* story."

"No, you don't," Fiona countered. "You're not interested in the truth. All you're interested in is the bounty on our heads and the gold it will bring you when we are delivered to Peabody."

Holt cocked his massive head a little to one side as he studied her closely. "Hmmm, she hears and reasons quite well and is actually smart. I like that! If you weren't so skinny and dirty, I might take a shine to you, Mrs. Moss. I'm hung like a horse and I could put my meat halfway up your shrunken belly, if I had a mind to rut with you some."

Inwardly, she shivered. Outwardly, she raised her chin and glared at Ransom Holt. "Don't you even think of touching me!"

"I would do more than touch you, if I found you attractive . . . which I definitely do not," Holt told her. "But

I can't say what Dalton and Eli will think once you get cleaned up and fattened a little."

"If you let them touch me, I'll kill myself!"

"No, you won't," Holt said with supreme confidence. "If you were of that mind, you'd already have done it when Jedediah and Ike were each raping you five or ten times a day and night in their dugout."

Fiona swallowed and knew that the man was right. She'd been raped over and over, humiliated, dirtied, and degraded so badly by the dead men lying nearby that nothing mattered. No one could hurt her any more than she'd already been hurt. She would endure anything to survive. To save Joe and to be reunited with their sweet daughter, Jessica.

"I'm right, aren't I," Ransom Holt said with satisfaction. "I could let Dalton and Eli rut on you any time they please and you wouldn't hurt yourself. And as for your husband, well, I'm damn sure that he's not going to be of much use to you either."

Fiona looked down at Joe. His breathing was shallow but regular. The bleeding was not nearly as severe as it had been, and she couldn't help but be amazed by the strength of his constitution . . . his sheer will to live.

"If you want the extra gold you'll get from Mr. Peabody for bringing my husband back to the Comstock Lode alive, then you have to get him to a doctor and give him time to mend."

"Don't be making demands on me, Mrs. Moss. I just hate to be told what to do."

"I'm sure that's true," Fiona said, "but I also know that you are greedy and you want all of Peabody's bounty gold."

He smiled and actually winked. "Just don't tell that to Dalton and his brother."

"I won't," she promised, "so long as you keep them away from me."

"That might not be possible."

"You can do it if you want," Fiona persisted. "You have to do it, or I will tell them you plan to murder them before they can reach the Comstock."

"You're only guessing at that," he said, voice hardening. "That's just crazy talk!"

"Is it, Mr. Holt? I just can't see someone like you sharing the bounty money."

"You don't know a thing about me, Fiona."

"I know all I need to know just from looking into your animal eyes," she replied with contempt.

His huge body tensed and he balled his fists. For a moment, she thought he was going to strike her down. And he was so large and powerful, and she now so weak and thin, that a single, well-delivered blow from his fist would likely have killed her. But at the last instant, Holt got control of himself and unclenched his big fists.

She stared into his feral eyes and he finally looked away. Deep inside her heart, Fiona knew that she had just won her first small, but important, victory and that Holt really would keep the brothers away from her already ravished and violated body.

"Don't ever come that close again to making me lose my temper," he warned. "If you do, I don't care how much money I'll lose because it'll be your pickled head that will arrive on the Comstock Lode."

Fiona nodded because she knew that he was telling her the truth and that she could never again push him quite so hard.

"Here are some rags," Dalton said, coming up to her. "Is he still alive?"

She took the dirty rags and began to stuff them into both the entry and exit wounds.

"Did he bleed out already?" Eli asked with mild curiosity.

"No, he did not," Fiona replied.

"Hey, boys!" Ransom Holt called. "Drag those scalped bodies into this dugout and let's set it afire."

"Why does he want us to do that?" Dalton whispered to his brother.

Overhearing this, Fiona whispered back, "Because Ransom Holt doesn't want to leave any trace of anyone who helps him in this bloody business."

"What is that supposed to mean?" Eli demanded.

Without bothering to look into their faces, Fiona said, "It means you had *both* better watch your own backs from now on."

The two exchanged quick glances, and then Dalton managed a short bark of a laugh. "You little whore! You're just trying to get into our minds. But you know what?"

"What?" she managed to ask.

"We're going to get into your pussy about as soon as we get finished burning those bodies."

Fiona froze with her blood turning to ice. She tried to summon up some bluster, but failed. Dalton reached out and put his hand on her breast. "There's still a little there to suck on. That's good!"

Suddenly, Fiona grabbed the bowie knife from her unconscious husband's sash and tried to bury its blade in Dalton's throat. But he was too quick for her and she had no strength. Twisting her wrist and tearing the knife away from Fiona, Dalton laughed. "You got a little fire left in the belly, huh, bitch? That's good, too."

Fiona shrank back. "If you touch me, Ransom Holt will kill you. He's going to kill you both anyway, but if you touch me before we get to Virginia City, he's going to kill you even sooner."

The brothers looked at one another and something passed between them. Then Eli actually whispered, "I suppose that could actually happen, bitch, if we don't kill Ransom Holt first."

So there it was. Fiona understood that before they reached the distant Comstock Lode, people were going to murder people in order to claim all of the bounty gold.

Once again, she saw a slender but definite ray of hope for herself and her husband, Joe Moss.

✛ 4 ✛

Fire was shooting out of the dugout, and Fiona listened to its roar, trying to ignore what she thought was a sizzling sound as the bodies of Jedediah Charles and Ike burned and boiled.

"Satisfied?" Ransom Holt asked. "Maybe now that I've disposed of those bodies so that the animals can't eat them, you'll actually view me as a human being."

Fiona almost shook her head, but caught herself in time. "Thank you for doing that. It was the Christian thing to do."

"Well, I'm no Christian and neither is anyone else here, so that doesn't matter much at all. Mostly, what I did it for is to eliminate any evidence or trace of that sorry pair."

"Joe's wound has closed, but he still needs a doctor," Fiona said, reminding Holt again.

"I've been thinking on that some," Holt replied. "And I think that Joe Moss is strong enough and you are a good enough nurse to keep him alive while we are on the move to the Comstock Lode."

"No!"

"My decision has been made," Holt said. "And I won't brook any arguments."

"Please be reasonable! My husband can't ride a horse! Look at him. He's pale and too weak from the loss of blood even to sit up."

"Yes," Holt said, "of that I am well aware."

"Then what—"

Holt cut off her question with a dismissive wave of his hand, then glanced over at the brothers. "Hey, boys, come on over here."

Dalton and Eli had been sorting through a few odds and ends they'd scavenged from the dugout, and now they sauntered over to look down at Joe Moss.

"He don't look too healthy," Eli said with an indifferent shrug. "Still think he's gonna make it?"

"He will," Fiona said. "If he gets a doctor and some bed rest."

"No doctor," Holt snapped. "And as for bed rest, well, that's what I wanted to talk to these boys about."

Dalton and Eli turned their attention to the big man.

"Boys," Holt said, "we're needing some supplies and a wagon."

The brothers frowned in serious concentration. Finally, Dalton said, "Why don't we git 'em on the way to Virginia City?"

"Because," Holt told him, "I don't want to deal with the Mormons and after we leave this part of the country, there isn't much of anything between us and the Comstock Lode except Paiute Indian villages."

"Paiute women sound good to me," Eli said with a cackle as he and Dalton leered at Fiona. "This 'un ain't gonna hold up too good with all three of us fucking her. She's way too skinny and weak."

Fiona colored and bit her lip. She was just thankful that

Joe Moss wasn't awake and aware of this conversation. If her husband had been awake, he'd have tried to kill all three despite his grave condition.

"Well, now," Holt said, towering over the leering brothers. "That brings up another issue. We're going to put Fiona and Joe Moss in shackles and keep them in locks and chains all the way across the desert."

"She ain't gonna have short leg shackles on so we can't squeeze in between them skinny legs, is she?" Dalton asked, his leer replaced by real concern. "Gotta give her enough chain to spread 'em wide."

"Can't do that," Holt said in his most genial voice. "We'll shackle both of them short—hand and foot."

"But . . ." Eli was forming a protest. "We'll all want to be fuckin' her!"

"No," Ransom said. "If you find some willing Paiute women, then you can have a go at them with my blessings, but Fiona is all mine."

"The hell you say!" Eli growled, hand moving toward the butt of his holstered six-gun.

"The hell I do say," Holt shot back, giving them a look that said there'd be no further argument.

"Fine," Dalton said. "I can wait for them Paiute women . . . or, I guess, even the whores up in Virginia City if it comes to that."

"Wise decision," Holt said, folding his massive arms across his chest. "You boys are gonna be pretty rich after Peabody pays us all off. You'll be able to buy the best whores money can buy . . . even the expensive ones in San Francisco."

"Yeah," Dalton said, not able to hide his great disappointment.

"All right, then," Holt told them. "As for Fiona, from the look of her right now, you'd have to pay me to fuck her."

It was meant as a joke and it went over well. Dalton and Eli guffawed and poked each other in the ribs, they were laughing so damned hard. Fiona just stared down at Joe and tried not to look even more ashamed than she felt. But deep inside, she knew that Ransom Holt had just eliminated one of her worst nightmares. She doubted that Joe could have endured being shackled and helpless while she was being raped all the way across Utah and Nevada.

"Now," Holt said, "let's talk about what we need in the way of provisions so we can get moving toward a big payday. First, we'll need a buckboard and a team of at least four good horses or mules. Also, I want a mattress for Joe Moss to lie on while—"

"A gawddamn mattress?" Eli cried in protest. "What the hell are we gonna let him ride on a mattress for!"

"So a long, rough trail in a buckboard doesn't open up those big holes in the front and back of his shoulder causing him to bleed to death," Holt explained.

Dalton and Eli both swore, but they could see the rationale for having a mattress under the badly wounded prisoner.

"The other things we need are food and supplies," Holt was telling them. "Lots of salt pork and beans, coffee, more ammunition in case we do have a problem with the Paiutes, and any other damn thing you can think of, including a few bottles of decent whiskey."

"I like that," Dalton said, licking his lips. "You frontin' the money for all this, boss?"

"Well, I know that you boys sure don't have any money, so I guess I'm stuck for it," Holt told them. "But you'd better be sharp about buying, and don't spend my money on liquor or women."

"Wouldn't think of that, now would we, Dalton?"

Dalton cackled. "Hell, no! We wouldn't dare waste any of the boss's money."

"See that you don't," Holt warned. "Because if you do, I'll take it out of your hides."

The brothers stopped their cackling and Eli asked, "How far do you reckon it is to Virginia City on the Comstock?"

Holt had a ready answer. "It's almost six hundred miles between where we're standing now and where Peabody is waiting to pay us all that gold. We'll be real lucky to make twenty or twenty-five miles a day with a buckboard, so that means the very best we can do is three weeks, but it's more likely it'll take a month of hard traveling."

Dalton and Eli considered those numbers, and reluctantly nodded their heads in agreement. "Sounds about right," the brothers both said.

"That's a mighty long ways," Dalton said. "We're gonna need a heap of supplies."

Holt dragged out a wallet and started counting greenbacks. He finished and handed Eli two hundred dollars. "And I'll want a written receipt for every damn dollar you spend."

"How about lettin' us have a little fun before we come back?" Dalton pleaded. "A few shots of whiskey. A woman for each of us."

"No," Holt said, eyes hard on the brothers. "Not one drop of whiskey and not one poke in a whore either. I want you to ride north to a little town called Placerville. I've been there before and the man at the general store is named Wakefield. Bert Wakefield."

"He your friend?"

Holt shook his head. "Let's just say that Bert knows better than to overcharge or cheat me. And I'm going to write out a list of supplies, and you'd better not add nor subtract anything from it."

"How many bottles of hooch?"

"Four," Holt said.

"Four?" the brothers cried. Dalton said, "Why, that pitiful amount of whiskey won't keep our gullets wet even past the Great Salt Lake!"

"All right," Holt said, already having decided that he would let them beat him up to six bottles. "Buy a half dozen."

"What about tobacco?"

"Buy a pound of it for yourselves," Holt said.

"And some licorice?"

"Hell, no!" Holt roared. "Dammit, I won't be bled to death buyin' you sorry sonofabitches candy!"

"All right!" Eli said. "No candy. No women. No whiskey in Placerville. Anything else we shouldn't do?"

"Don't take your time," Holt told them. "I want you boys back here with the supplies loaded in a good buckboard with a mattress and four strong horses in three days or less."

"Don't think two hundred will buy all you're askin' for," Eli told him.

"It will," Holt said. "Make sure of it."

The brothers nodded and turned away to get their horses.

"What happens here during the next three days?" Fiona asked.

Holt looked at her. "Nothing except you get your man ready for traveling."

"I don't even have any medicines or clean bandages."

"Boil some rags and find some grease or fat. I don't care. Just get Joe Moss ready to go."

Fiona nodded. "It's a long, dangerous road to Virginia City. Lots of desert and Paiute Indians and not much water."

"So why are you telling me what I already know?" the big man asked.

"I just wanted to warn you," Fiona said. "There's a good chance that we could be killed by the Indians or die of thirst."

"Let me be the one to worry about that," Holt told her.

"You just get Joe Moss healthy enough to ride in a buckboard for six hundred miles."

Fiona turned back to her man and smoothed his brow as Holt went off to write his supply list. "Joe, Joe," she crooned softly. "I know you can't hear me right now, but we're in a terrible fix."

One of Joe's eyelids popped open and he even managed a weak smile before he whispered. "Don't you worry, little darlin'. We're gonna kill Holt and be ready for them other two bastards when they come back with a wagon and supplies."

Fiona was astonished! She could hardly believe that her husband was awake and aware. Suddenly, she felt as if a terrible weight had been lifted from her thin shoulders.

"Yes," she whispered, squeezing Joe's pale hand for all she was worth. "We'll kill him and then we'll kill the other two!"

"They're as good as dead right now," Joe softly told her, closing his eye and drifting back to sleep.

✦ 5 ✦

AFTER THE BROTHERS had left for Placerville, Fiona tried to appear busy and defeated. She knew that her Joe was drifting in and out of sleep and that he was in no condition to try to kill Ransom Holt just yet. But if he had three days before the brothers returned with a wagon and supplies, well, maybe Joe could sit up and use a gun or even his knife to catch Holt by surprise and kill him quick.

And I can help Joe do that, she told herself. *I can help him kill that big man, and then we'll deal with the brothers when they ride up on the wagon. Afterward, we'll use all those supplies and horses to take us to Virginia City to collect our daughter, Jessica.*

"So how is Joe doing?" Holt asked her the second day. "Any sign that your husband is coming around?"

"Not yet," Fiona lied. "Joe lost so much blood, he might stay unconscious for another day or two."

· "That doesn't sound right to me," Holt said with a frown. "I've shot and killed plenty of men and they either die . . . or they wake up screamin' and moanin'. Are you *sure* Joe is still out cold?"

Fiona tried to look him in the eye when she said, "Of course I am!"

"We'll see," Holt said, drawing his pistol and starting toward Joe Moss.

"What are you going to do!" Fiona cried, running around in front of the giant, trying to block his path. "What are you going to do to Joe!"

"I'm gonna wake him up," Moss spat. "Now stand aside, woman."

"No, please!"

Holt backhanded her hard enough to send Fiona sprawling. Then he marched up to Joe Moss and cocked his gun. "Open your eyes, you sonofabitch, or I'll shoot your balls off right now!"

Joe didn't move or open his eyes.

"Okay," Holt said, cocking back the hammer of his gun. "I'm gonna castrate you with bullets!"

Holt fired, and the bullet struck the dirt right under Joe's crotch. Joe jumped and tried to kick out with a leg and trip the big man, but he was so weak that he failed, and then he tried to get up and fight, but couldn't.

Fiona threw herself at Holt, but he slapped her down to the dirt again and looked amused at their failed trickery.

"My, oh, my!" Holt crowed as he stepped back. "Look at what we got here. A man pretending to be almost dead suddenly wakes up fighting mad!"

Joe was breathing hard and feeling weaker than a kitten, but even so he made a grab for his bowie knife, only to discover that it was gone.

"All right," Holt said. "Pretend time is over. Moss, tell

your woman she had better not try to attack me again or I'll kill her on the spot."

Joe's mouth was so dry and his voice so weak that he didn't even try to respond to that threat.

"Fiona, you go get your chains and shackles lyin' over there in the dirt. The ones you wore when Jedediah and Ike had you all to themselves. Then I want you to chain yourself to your husband."

"But . . . but how am I supposed to tend to his wounds if . . ."

"Figure it out, you skinny slut!"

Holt turned his gun on her and for just a moment, Fiona was sure that he was going to go berserk and kill her right then and there. "All right! All right," she cried, scrambling to her feet and running to retrieve the hated chains and shackles she'd been wearing for weeks.

"Put 'em on tight. Attach your right leg to his left leg. Your right arm to his left arm. That's it. Nice and tight."

When they were shackled together side by side lying in the dirt, all the hope that Fiona had been secretly carrying in her heart bled away and she began to cry.

Joe cleared his throat and whispered, "This ain't the end of us, Fiona. Just because we had a little setback here don't mean we're whipped. Don't give up on us."

Fiona nodded through her tears, but she was beginning to think that their string of terrible luck just wasn't ever going to end and they would eventually wind up swinging from a rope in distant Virginia City.

"Hang on to your senses," Joe urged, trying to squeeze her hand. "I've been in worse fixes than this and come out alive."

"But you've never been chained to me in such a near-hopeless fix as we're in right now."

"Bein' chained to you makes it all easier," he lied. "Makes it more of a challenge maybe, but easier somehow."

"I don't understand that," she replied.

"It don't matter, Fiona. The thing of it is that you just keep believin' that we're gonna make it out of this alive and someday have our daughter and live happy all together."

"Are you serious, Joe? You sure you're not just telling me that to make me feel better until we either get killed by Holt or hanged by Peabody?"

"I'm dead serious," Joe whispered. "Dead *damned* serious!"

Fiona nodded, trying her very best just to believe. She *had* to believe. Otherwise, she was going to go mad, and then how would Joe ever survive being shackled to a crazy woman?

That night Ransom Holt built a bonfire and dragged Joe and Fiona closer to the fire. "There's a chill in the air and you two are worth a whole lot more to me alive than dead," he explained as he uncorked a bottle of whiskey, pulled up a blanket, and enjoyed his fire.

Holt tilted the bottle up to the stars and drank deeply. He sighed with contentment and smiled, his meaty face highlighted by the flames. "I have always enjoyed a good, big fire," he told his two prisoners. "When I was a boy growing up on a farm in Connecticut, I would build bonfires out of the tree stumps that we used to pull out to clear our fields. I'd sneak some kerosene out of my father's shed and drench those stumps, then pile dead branches and leaves all around them and set 'em afire! Lordy, but they burned high and bright. I'd dance around the flames pretending I was a wild Indian. I'd whoop and holler and have the best old time."

Holt took another drink, and it was clear that he wanted to go back in time and to reminisce. "My father was a circus freak," he admitted. "He was an inch taller than I am now and thicker. He could lift a fully grown horse right off the damned ground, and he did all sorts of lifting feats for suckers who would pay to watch. Sometimes, he'd wrestle three or four men at a time for a purse. He never lost. My father was big, strong, and mean as a snake. He'd whip me just for the hell of it, and he'd whip my mother until she begged him to stop."

Fiona looked sideways at Holt. "Why didn't your mother take you and run away?"

"Oh," Ransom Holt said, still gazing deep into the flames. "She tried that once. But only once, because he broke her leg over his knee and then he smashed her kneecap with a hammer, shattering it all to hell so the best that she could do was hobble."

Holt's voice was taking on rage. "My father broke Mother's leg and kneecap, telling her that he would break her neck and mine the next time she tried to run away with me. And he wasn't bluffing."

Fiona knew she shouldn't say another word, but something made her blurt, "What eventually happened to your father?"

"Well," Holt said, suddenly grinning after taking another long pull on his bottle, "came the day I was sixteen and my father got drunk and brought home a young little whore not much bigger than you. He fucked her right in front of my mother, laughing all the time he did it, and then he told my mother to undress."

Fiona swallowed hard. "Why would he do such a thing?"

"He ordered her to undress because she was old and beat up and not good to look at anymore." Holt's lips twisted with hate. "My mother protested, and then Father began to beat her in front of the naked whore. When my mother couldn't take any more, she started to remove the only old dress she owned, and that's when something inside me just . . . just snapped. I went crazy."

Holt threw down his whiskey and his eyes tightened and his lips formed a thin, white slash across his face. "There was a hatchet resting by our fireplace, and I grabbed it up and started slashing at my father. He was strong, but he wasn't made of steel, and when I chopped off his hand, he lost his nerve, and that's when I split his head open from the hairline right down to his filthy mouth."

"That's what I'd have done, too," Joe Moss said. "Only, I wouldn't have waited until I was sixteen years old. I'd have killed that old bastard when I was twelve."

Holt glanced at Joe and actually smiled. "I'm sure you would have tried. But then you got more guts than anyone I ever knew and you're about half crazy when it comes to killing. The truth is that you wouldn't have had a chance against my old man at twelve years old any more than I did. So I waited and got him killed at sixteen."

"What about the little woman he had that night?" Fiona asked.

"I killed that little whore, too."

"Why'd you do that?" Joe asked.

"Because when my mother had to take off her dress, the little whore pointed at Mother's fat, sagging body and started to giggle. You see, she was making fun of my mother's body and I just couldn't abide that."

"Did you also hack her to death?" Fiona asked.

"Naw," Holt said, taking a drink. "I dragged her out to the barn and fucked her, then I beat her brains out with a singletree."

Fiona shuddered.

"And then you know what I did?" Holt asked the fire.

"What?" Joe asked.

"I killed my mother because she was so miserable. But I killed her quick and easy and she asked me to do it. I didn't want to at first because I loved her, but she begged me to kill her, so I finally did. I buried Mother, but I lit the barn on fire with my father and the whore inside."

"And then?" Fiona asked quietly.

"Then I ran away and never looked back. I started bare-knuckle fighting for prize money. I'm so big that there were few foolish enough to get into a ring with me, so I'd take on two or three at a time just like my father had done. And I'd always win. Always."

Holt took another drink. "I did that until I beat a man to death in the ring in Chicago. They tried to arrest me, and I decided I had better get out of town and keep movin' or I might get hanged. You see, the young fella that I beat to death was well connected to some dangerous people."

Holt laughed to himself and shook his head. "I didn't even get to collect the purse I'd won that night in Chicago, but it didn't matter. I have always been able to get work killing someone for money, or else protecting some rich sonofabitch from his enemies."

"So you learned to shoot and use a knife?" Joe asked, knowing this information would be very important to him in the future.

"Oh, yeah," Holt said, looking at Joe. "I learned how to use a gun, a rifle, a knife, and everything else that kills. However, I never learned how to use a tomahawk to kill and scalp men like you do, Joe."

"I could teach you," Joe offered. "Take off these shackles and we'll give it a few practice throws right now."

Holt laughed without mirth. "Yeah, I'll just bet you'd like to do that. Yeah, you sure as hell would! And I'd wind up with your tomahawk stuck in my forehead."

Holt stopped laughing and took another pull on the bottle. He glanced over at Joe and Fiona and said, "I'll tell you both a little secret."

"Maybe we don't want to hear it," Joe told the big man.

"Sure you do," Holt assured them. "Because the secret is that I admire you, Joe. I admire how tough you are and how many of the informants I've paid to keep looking for you are dead by your hand."

"How much did you pay 'em for watchin' out for me all these months?"

"Not much. Ten dollars, but they stood to make a hundred if they saw you and got word to me fast enough to find you."

"Ten dollars, huh," Joe mused. "Not much to die for."

"Men have died for a lot less," Holt said. "So how many of 'em did you kill, Joe?"

Joe thought about that. "Four or five."

"And you took their scalps?"

"I did," Joe said with honest pride. "But Fiona don't like the look or smell of them, so I gave 'em up."

"You should have kept them," Holt told him. "I'd have liked to have them myself."

"Why'd you want to have scalps that you didn't even take?" Joe asked with genuine curiosity.

"Well," Holt mused, his eyelids getting heavy. "Maybe I wouldn't have. I don't know. The scalp taking is new to me. I'll have to give that one some thought."

"Do that," Joe told the man. "And maybe you ought to give some thought about what you plan to do to us."

"There isn't any thinking required," Holt replied with a yawn. "I promised Peabody that I'd bring you both in dead or alive. Preferably alive. And that's exactly what I intend to do."

"Long ways to Nevada," Joe commented.

"Yep, sure is. But in one month we'll be there and this business will all be over with. That'll be quite a necktie party on the Comstock, Joe. Most have seen men swing, but not many have seen a woman dance in the air."

"Fiona isn't going to hang," Joe vowed, his voice sharp and cold. "If I get hanged, well, I sorta deserve it. But she don't."

"Deserving or not, she'll hang right with you, Joe. You better wrap your mind around that here and now."

"I don't I think I will," Joe told him. "And like I said, it's a long way to Virginia City. You speak any Paiute?"

"Hell, no."

"I do . . . a little," Joe told him. "I speak most all the Indian languages, or enough of each to get my meaning across. Sign language if everything else fails and their blood is up."

"I'm not afraid of the Paiutes," Holt told him. "They're a filthy rabble that eats lizards, grubs, and whatever else they can manage to get down their gullets. It's not like I've got to get you through Cheyenne or Blackfoot land."

"Maybe not," Joe agreed. "But the Paiute will fight. And we're a small party . . . given that I'll be shackled. You think that Dalton and Eli are going to stand up to being attacked by Indians?"

"They'll stand and fight. Those boys are killers."

"Yeah, I suppose they are," Joe said, "but I also 'spect they're back-shooters and drunk-robbers. Men used to having the advantage all the time. But out there in the desert against the Paiutes, they might just lose their nerve."

"If they do, then we'll all probably die," Holt said. "Either way, there's no sense in worrying about it until it happens. But I'm confident we can get to the Comstock Lode. After that, my life is going to be way different."

"How's that?" Joe asked.

Holt was almost through with his bottle. "After I am paid off by Garrison Peabody, I'm going to go to San Francisco and live like a king for a month or two. When I start to get tired of that, I'm going to buy passage to the Sandwich Islands and live by the sea with a couple of native girls. Just swim, fuck, eat fish and coconuts, and sleep in a nice grass hut. You ever even hear of those islands, Joe?"

"Hell, no."

"I didn't think so," Holt told him. "I've read about them in magazines and even seen a few pictures. Ain't nothin' prettier in this world. I'll be putting all my past behind me and I'll keep enough money to live with those natives like I was their big king."

"You don't seem like the type to be happy eatin' nuts and sleepin' under tree limbs and branches," Joe said. "But it don't matter because you'll never live to find out."

Holt drained his bottle and turned his burning red eyes on Joe Moss. "It's true that you're both worth more to me alive than dead. But here's something that's also true and that you'd best remember. Just don't you get too mouthy with me, or I'll start fucking your wife right in front of your face."

Joe's face went bone white, and he had to bite his tongue until it bled in order not to say something that could get him killed by a man who was more than half drunk. Finally, he was able to speak and said, "To do that you'd have to unshackle me from her. And, Holt, when you did that, I'd find a way to kill you."

"No, you wouldn't. Because I'd cut off your balls and you'd be so busy trying to hang on to your crotch that you wouldn't care what I did to your skinny little wife."

Joe's eyes blazed and he didn't dare say another word. But he would keep this conversation and these crude insults to his Fiona well in mind for a future time when he had the advantage over this man. Yes, he'd remember Ransom Holt's every dirty word when he scalped and then skinned him alive.

"ARE WE REALLY goin' all the way to Placerville to get supplies?" Dalton asked his older brother as they topped a steep, rocky ridge and dismounted to stretch their legs and let their horses blow.

"I don't see that we got much choice," Eli replied.

"We could just keep going with Holt's two hundred dollars."

"Yeah," Eli said, checking his cinch, "we could do that. Of course, Ransom Holt would pay someone to find and ambush us . . . if he didn't track us down and then kill us slow all by himself."

"I'm not afraid of Ransom Holt," Dalton declared, patting the big double-barreled shotgun on his saddle. "Sure he's big and hard, but there ain't no man can stand up against this shotgun. No man alive."

Eli nodded. "I know that, but Ransom Holt has this all figured out. If we deliver Joe Moss and his little whore to Peabody, you and I have been promised a thousand dollars."

"A thousand dollars is a heap of gold, but we both know that Holt will get a lot more for his share," Dalton said hotly.

"That's true, but he's the boss." Eli smiled. "And we've already decided to kill Holt just before we get to Virginia City and have all the bounty money. But to just run off with Holt's supply money right now, well, that seems sorta dumb to me."

"Yeah," Dalton said, "I guess it is at that. But Holt is really gettin' on my nerves. He thinks he walks on water and is smarter than all the rest of us put together."

"I know," Eli said, trying to appease his hotheaded younger brother, "but we can't forget that the big man is damned dangerous. We're gonna have to play along with his game until we get near the Comstock Lode, and then we'll have to be real careful about making our move and killing him . . . because I suspect he's gonna figure our game out long before we get across those deserts."

Dalton's brow furrowed. "Do you think so, brother?"

"I'm sure of it," Eli replied. "And I wouldn't doubt that he's plannin' to do the same to us as we're plannin' to do to him."

Dalton nodded grimly. "So that's the game we're caught up in right now?"

"I believe it is," Eli said to his kid brother. "Kill or be killed, providin' we survive the desert and the Paiutes."

Dalton sighed. "We just have to keep reminding ourselves about that thousand dollars for each of us, and a lot more if we kill Holt and take Moss and his woman into Virginia City shackled."

"We can do this," Eli said with confidence. "Do you remember when Holt told us that he wanted to go to the Sandwich Islands and screw native girls and sleep on the beach once he gets his money from Peabody?"

"Sure do," Dalton said with derision. "That big man is gonna sleep all right, but it'll be six feet deep under Nevada sagebrush." Dalton chuckled. "I just got me an idea."

"Let's hear it."

"We don't have to go all the way to Placerville and buy supplies from Ransom Holt's friend who owns a general store."

"No? Why not?"

"Because there's bound to be a Mormon settlement around here with a general store. I'm thinking we ought to find it and then rob it."

"What about the buckboard and team of horses?" Eli asked. "Be kinda tough to steal them right out of the middle of some Mormon town."

"It can be done," Dalton insisted. "We just have to find us a little town and sneak into it late at night. First we steal the wagon and horses, and then we drive 'em up to the back of the Mormon general store and bust in the back door. We load up and get everything Holt put on his list and drive off! Holt will never know where we got the supplies, wagon, and horses and we can pocket his two hundred dollars."

"Hmmm," Eli said, "that ain't such a bad idea."

"It's a great idea!"

"So we just have to find a settlement with a livery and general store."

"That's right," Dalton said, excitement growing in his voice. "From what I've seen, Mormons ain't nothin' but a bunch of farmers that couldn't put up much of a fight even if we robbed 'em in broad daylight. They'd probably just fall on their Bibles or whatever they read and pray for old Brigham Young himself to come and save 'em!"

"All right," Eli said, "so let's see if we can find us a little Mormon town before we get to Placerville."

"If we don't," Dalton told him, "we'll just rob Holt's friend in Placerville and steal a local wagon and horses."

"Sounds good to me," Eli said, jamming a boot into his stirrup. "Let's do it."

Late that afternoon, they came upon a small farming community called Moroni. Eli and Dalton drew their horses up about a mile south of the town and studied it for a while.

"Well," Dalton finally said, "what do you think?"

"There looks to be maybe five hundred farmers and their families living there," Eli said. "And from the appearance of the town, I'd say they'll most likely have a general store and livery that we can rob."

Dalton slapped his hand down on his saddle horn. "Then this is good enough. How should we play this out?"

"We ride into those pines yonder," Eli said, "and take a nap until it gets late. Then we wait until midnight, go into Moroni, and steal a wagon and team of horses. After we got the buckboard hitched, we back it up to their general store, bust in, and take what Holt's list says we need in the way of supplies. Dalton, I don't think it could get much simpler."

"I could use a long nap," Dalton said. "But I could use a pretty Mormon girl even more."

"Forget that!" Eli snapped. "They may be just a bunch of cow-shit farmers, but they still might have a few old rifles loaded and ready to use and we don't need that kind of trouble."

"All right," Dalton said, reining his horse toward the trees. "But how are we goin' to get a mattress if we don't see a woman?"

"Hmmm," Eli said, "I'd forgotten all about the damned mattress Holt wanted us to buy. To hell with it! We can fill the buckboard with some straw. That ought to be good enough for the likes of Joe Moss. Now let's get some shut-eye and then rob the farmers so's we can keep Holt's money without him bein' none the wiser."

Dalton chuckled. "Be good to put one over on Holt. That man is just way too high-and-mighty."

"Amen," Eli said in ready agreement.

They waited until almost midnight before they quietly rode into Moroni and found both the town's livery and general store. It was a pitch-dark, nearly moonless night, and everything was going in their favor. Dalton and Eli tied their horses up to a corral full of farm and riding horses, lit a match, and found halters, ropes, and harness neatly hanging on pegs just inside the barn door.

"There ain't nobody sleepin' in this barn," Eli said, locating a lantern and turning the wick down low. "Easy, easy pickin's."

"The owner probably lives in that house just across the yard. He's sleepin' away with his wife, and won't he be surprised come morning when he counts his horses and finds four missin' along with his best buckboard."

The brothers giggled like a couple of schoolboys playing a trick on their unsuspecting teacher.

"Let's harness four of the biggest horses and get that buckboard hitched up," Dalton said.

The brothers were good with horses, and they had no trouble getting them collected and then harnessed and hitched. They tied their own saddled mounts to the back of the buckboard, and led the team around to the rear of the general store. As they went about their thievery, there was not a sound in the village and not a light in any cabin window.

"It's all goin' good," Dalton said.

"Better'n good," Eli said, taking a little hammer and

chisel that he'd found in the livery and going to work on the flimsy hasp and lock that secured the back door of the general store.

But when the hammer struck and the chisel pried the hasp partway out of the wooden doorjamb, there was a loud shriek of protest. Somewhere not far away, a couple of town dogs began to bark.

Dalton and Eli froze and listened for voices. Both had their knives in their hands, and they were ready to silence anyone who came to investigate.

The dogs stopped barking and the town of Moroni slept blissfully and totally unaware.

"It's all right," Eli assured his brother. "Let's get that door open and get the wagon loaded. I'm gonna steal a lot more than six bottles of whiskey."

"Shit!" Dalton swore. "There ain't gonna be no whiskey here! This is a *Mormon* town and those dumb bastards don't drink liquor."

"Shit! You're right," Eli said.

"How are we gonna explain no whiskey to Holt? And these sonsabitches won't have any tobacco neither!" Dalton's voice was filled with disappointment.

"Damned if I know what we'll tell Holt. We'll worry about that when the time comes. Let's get this business finished and leave this farmin' town. I'm startin' to get jumpy."

"Me, too," Dalton admitted.

The brothers finally broke in through the back door, and after stumbling around in the dark, lit matches and found feed sacks to stuff provisions into. They didn't take the time nor go to the bother of consulting Holt's carefully written shopping list. They'd read the list over a number of times and pretty much knew it by heart. Now they began to load the wagon, and when that was done, they searched high and low for some extra ammunition and weapons, but didn't find any.

"These farmers must not abide weapons any more than they do liquor or tobacco," Dalton observed.

"It would seem that way," his brother replied. "Are we all loaded up and ready to go?"

"Yep."

"Then let's get out of here," Eli ordered. "A general store without rotgut or tobacco is a sorry place, and I sure wish we could have found some more guns, rifles, and ammunition just in case we are jumped by the Paiutes."

"Me, too," Dalton said. "And I couldn't even find no damned coffee. Don't they like coffee either?"

"Maybe not," Eli said. "These are strange people."

"Amen."

The brothers hastily piled into the loaded buckboard and started out of town. But one of the horses, a big gray gelding, apparently had never been in harness and was strictly a riding animal. Right away, it began to fight and buck. It raised so much of a fuss that two of the boxes of provisions spilled out of the back of the buckboard and crashed in the back alley.

Then the dogs of Moroni started barking again, and one actually came running out from under a porch. It wasn't very big, just a runty little thing, but it was angry and it flew at the team of horses, biting one on the fetlock.

Suddenly, two horses were bucking and rearing, and then Dalton swore and drew his gun and was ready to shoot the little dog.

"No, gawddammit! You'll wake up the whole damn town!"

"Looks like it's already startin' to come awake," Dalton said, holstering his six-gun. "Lights comin' on in windows all over the place."

Eli felt a deep sense of dread, and he slapped the lines

down hard on the back of the four-horse team. "Ya!" he hissed.

The team lunged forward into a crazy run. Boxes of provisions bounced off the wagon and broke open in their wake, and over the pounding of hoofbeats both Dalton and Eli heard angry shouts.

"You think they're comin' after us?" Dalton called, clutching the shotgun and looking nervously back over his shoulder at boxes smashing on the road just behind, causing their two saddle horses to break loose and gallop off into the dark night.

"Naw!" Eli called back. "They're just a bunch of chickenshit Mormon farmers without guns, whiskey, or tobacco. They won't do jack shit!"

"I sure hope you're right. Our saddle horses just broke loose and run off, so we're kinda in a fix if we have to get away fast."

The brothers exchanged glances, and it was probably a good thing it was so dark and neither one could see the other's fear.

"Where the hell did the road go!" Dalton shouted as the wagon began to jump and buck wildly across a freshly plowed field. "All the gawddamn supplies are bouncin' out the back of this buckboard! We're gonna end up with nothin'!"

Eli knew that was the truth, so he finally got the team down to a walk. He set the brake on the wagon and jumped down to calm the sweating team of horses. "Dalton, push everything left up to the front of the wagon."

"All right."

"How much of that stuff from the general store did we lose?"

"As near as I can tell, we lost about half of it," Dalton

answered. "Damn it to hell! We'd have been better off just to mosey out of Moroni and if those Mormons came after us wantin' a fight, we could have killed 'em and taken their horses and guns."

"There might have been more than even we could handle," Eli told him.

"Where in the hell are we?"

"Some farmer's cornfield, I reckon."

"Shit! Now what are we gonna do?"

"Quiet," Eli said. "I need to think this out."

After a few minutes, Dalton hissed, "Eli, do you hear the sound of hoofbeats comin'? Sounds like the whole damned cavalry!"

"Uh-oh," Eli said. "See them lanterns way back there toward town? Them stupid Mormon bastards are following us."

"What are we gonna do!"

"I reckon we'll move on and see if we can find a place to make a stand come daylight," Eli decided after a long pause. "But maybe they'll get smart and go back to town."

"I don't know," Dalton fretted. "I think they're really after us."

"Well," Eli told his younger brother, "if they want to get their tickets to Hell punched come morning, I'm sure we can oblige them."

"Yeah, we can do that. But I'm a little low on shotgun shells."

"How about your pistol?"

"I'm in pretty good shape for ammunition."

"Me, too. And I've got the Sharps." Eli groped his way back into the seat of the buckboard and felt his brother do the same. Squinting into the night, he said, "I think there's a barn and house up ahead. Maybe we ought to pull up behind the barn and use it for cover to hide."

"I dunno. I'm thinking we should just keep moving as

fast as this damn wagon can travel," Dalton said. "I sure wish we hadn't lost our horses and saddles."

"Yeah, and with this buckboard bouncin' across these cornfields, we damned sure ain't gonna get us anyplace quick. Dalton, I still think that we ought to hide behind that hay barn."

"Whatever you think, big brother. I sure wish we had our saddle horses, though."

"Me, too, but let's just deal with the cards we're holdin' and I reckon everything will turn out just fine."

"I hope so," Dalton said, trying to hide his worry. "I really ain't got anything against those stupid Mormon farmers. Don't even want to kill 'em especially."

"Want may have nothing to do with it," Eli said. "If they come for us, we'll kill 'em to the last farmer."

"That we will," Dalton agreed as his brother slowly drove the buckboard toward the dim outline of a big wooden hay barn.

✛ 7 ✛

"THOSE LIGHTS ARE gettin' closer!" Dalton said as he jumped down from the buckboard and peered around the barn. "Can't be more than a mile off now. Eli, maybe we should keep movin'."

"I'm not sure what we should do," Eli confessed. "Last damn thing in the world I expected was a bunch of Mormon farmers comin' after us."

"There's a *lot* of lights! Must be thirty or forty just bobbin' along in the dark like a swarm of fireflies! But they're gettin' closer and closer. You think they got guns, Eli?"

"I expect that's possible."

"But they're just *farmers*! They probably can't hit this barn with those guns or rifles."

"That's right," Eli agreed. "They're just farmers who can't shoot straight and have lost their senses coming after two like us."

"They're dumb farmers that are gonna get themselves killed!"

"Yeah," Eli agreed. "But maybe we ought to unhitch

those horses from the buckboard and see if we can find any saddles or bridles in this barn."

Dalton was astonished by the suggestion. "You mean just leave the buckboard and what provisions that didn't spill out the back of it?"

"I'm not saying that we're going to have to do that," Eli told him, trying to sound calm. "I'm just saying that we ought to saddle a couple of horses just in case."

"In case all those Mormons can shoot straight?" Dalton felt sweat trickling down his backbone even though the night was cool. "Stealing supplies from a general store will get us long jail time, Eli. But stealing horses will get us both *hanged*. I ain't gonna swing! No, sir! Not from no Mormon rope and not from any other damned rope either!"

"They're almost a mile away," Eli said, "so let's calm down and see if we can find saddles and bridles. I don't expect we'll have to use them, but it would be stupid not to have horses ready just in case things go worse than expected."

"I'll go search the barn," Dalton said, sliding along its rough side. "Sure wish that it wasn't so damned dark!"

"There has to be a lantern in the barn. You've got matches?"

"Sure."

"All right," Eli said. "Don't waste any time in there. We need to get a couple of horses saddled . . . just in case."

"Yeah, just in case."

Eli stood at the corner of the barn trying to ignore the pounding of his heart. He clutched the heavy Sharps rifle, and knew that he could hit any of those dancing firefly lights when they came upon the plowed field. But he was hoping that somehow he wouldn't have to do that. If he killed farmers, they might become that much more determined for justice and hang him and Dalton for certain. But, dammit, they were still coming and somehow they had to be stopped!

It seemed to take forever before Dalton stumbled out of the cavernous barn and announced, "No saddles, brother, but I found a pair of halters that we could use to make bridles and reins. Jeezus, they're really getting close now!"

"Ignore their lanterns and cut loose that fractious gray horse that was giving us so much trouble leaving Moroni."

"But he's probably the only true saddle horse of the four!" Dalton protested.

"He's fractious and too high-spirited to ride bareback without even a bit between his teeth. He'd likely start bucking if you jumped on him."

"No!" Dalton cried. "He's the best horse of the four. The only one that looks like he has any speed. He's the one that I'll ride, if we have to make a run for it."

Eli knew that there were times when it was impossible to argue with his younger brother. Dalton would get his back up and become so stubborn that he'd do what he'd do no matter what was said or done.

"All right," Eli told his brother. "Halter that big gray horse for yourself and then halter that black one for me to ride."

"Just in case."

"Yeah, just in case. Bit 'em with the rope around the jaw Indian style and hurry it up!"

"Okay," Dalton said. "You gonna start shooting pretty quick? They're in the range of your Sharps now."

"I'm gonna fire a shot over their heads and scatter them," Eli told his brother. "After they hear the roar of this big buffalo rifle, I'm sure that they'll turn tail and run back to Moroni."

Dalton actually giggled. "Sure they will! Why, I sure

wish I could stand and watch them lights disappearin' in the dark."

"Just get the gray and the black haltered and Indian-bitted," Eli said, raising the Sharps rifle and taking aim at a spot maybe twenty yards in front of the lead light.

He fired, and two bad things instantly happened. His slug must have struck a field rock and ricocheted upward, because one of the lights dropped and a Mormon screamed. And right after that, the gray horse reared and knocked Dalton into the barn wall with such force that Eli knew that his younger brother would be stunned, maybe even hurt.

Eli turned and saw Dalton stagger and somehow manage to hang on to the lead ropes of the two chosen escape horses.

"You all right?" Eli asked.

"Yeah, I guess. A little woozy, but I'll be all right. Are they all runnin' away, Eli? Are they all runnin' back to Moroni like scared rabbits?"

"No."

"Well, well, what did they do?"

"They doused their lights and I can't see any of them out there anymore."

"Well, that must be because they're running back to town!" Dalton cried.

"I don't think so," Eli told him. "I think they're creeping up on us while staying low in the corn rows."

"But—"

Whatever Dalton was about to ask was interrupted by a fusillade of bullets and muzzle flashes. Both brothers heard the volley of slugs slam into the hay barn they were hiding behind.

"They're going to come for us," Eli said. "They've no intention of running back to town."

Dalton moaned, then managed to ask, "All of 'em, you think?"

"Yeah, except maybe the one that I accidentally hit with a ricochet."

"Well, we can't stand up against *all* of 'em."

"I know that, dammit! We're gonna have to get on those horses and make a run for it and we'd better do it right now."

"Shit!" Dalton cried.

"Let's go!"

Eli grabbed the lead rope to the black horse he'd chosen to ride, and he looped it to make reins. It wasn't a big horse, but it was stout and looked to be strong and willing. It wasn't easy for him to swing up on the black with the Sharps rifle, but somehow he managed.

"Come on, Dalton!"

Dalton was hurt, woozy, but desperately trying to mount the fractious gray and still keep hold of the double-barreled shotgun. But the gray was jumping around and it was a tall horse. Too tall for Dalton to swing up onto with the shotgun gripped in one hand and his head spinning crazily.

"Drop the shotgun and get on that horse!" Eli shouted as rifle shots opened up like winking cats' eyes in the fields. The muzzle flashes were a lot closer than they had been, and that told Eli that the Mormons had been rapidly crawling across the field to get into firing range. "Come on, Dalton, drop your gawddamn shotgun and swing onto that damned gray horse because those Mormons are comin' for us!"

But Dalton was hurt, angry, and scared, and he was fighting with the gray horse. He tried to hit the gray in the head with the barrel of the shotgun, and missed. The shotgun flew out into the darkness. Dalton cursed and then grabbed the gray's mane, and somehow finally swung onto the animal's back. But it reared up into the air and out of the corner of his eye, Eli saw the crazed animal fall over backward.

"Dalton!"

The Mormon rifles were firing again, and bullets were cutting the air like wasps all around Eli. One clipped his black's ear and the frightened animal almost spun out from under Eli, dumping him. The gray horse scrambled off Dalton's writhing body and bolted into the night. The other two stolen horses still hitched to the buckboard began to fight and surge against the brake.

"Ahhh!" Dalton screamed as the iron-rimmed wheels of the buckboard skidded across his lower legs. "Oh, gawd! Oh, gawd!"

Eli wanted to jump down and help his kid brother. But the bullets were flying everywhere and he knew that there was no time left to be a hero. Either he ran . . . or he died!

"Eli, don't leave me!"

Eli drove his heels into the flanks of the black and sent it flying away from the barn. His fingers were laced in the animal's mane, and in his other hand he held the heavy Sharps rifle.

He thought he heard his brother calling. . . . no, screaming . . . his name, but he shut out the sound and concentrated on riding to save his life.

There were two or three more shots from behind the barn and then silence. Silence except for the blood pounding in Eli's ears, racing even faster than the black's flying hooves.

✣ **8** ✣

"SOMEONE IS COMING," Joe Moss announced. "But it's probably not Dalton and Eli because this one is alone and riding a black horse without a saddle."

Ransom Holt picked up his rifle and waited.

"Is it a Paiute?" Fiona asked, squinting into the afternoon sun.

"Nope," Joe told her. "Paiutes ride better'n this fella and they're usually smaller."

"It's Eli," Ransom announced with disgust. "Dammit, something must have gone wrong in Placerville!"

Joe and Fiona, shackled and chained, stood and waited along with Ransom Holt. When Eli finally reined the sweating horse in and slipped off its bare back, he staggered and then collapsed, still holding the Sharps rifle but having little else on his person.

"What happened?" Ransom Holt demanded, towering over the exhausted man. "Where's your brother and the horses you left here on?"

"We got into a terrible fix," Eli said, shaking his head. "Ran into trouble in Placerville and—"

Holt reached down and jerked the smaller man to his feet and shook him hard. "What kind of fucking trouble? Where's your brother, where's my buckboard and supplies, and since you don't have any of them, where the hell is my two hundred dollars?"

"I still got it! I got it right here," Eli stammered. "We didn't go on a drinkin' spree or piss your money away on whores or anything, Mr. Holt! I swear we didn't."

Holt shoved the man backward. "Then what did happen?"

Eli swallowed. "Well, sir, it was like this. We was on our way to Placerville when some Indians jumped us and took everything including our horses."

"What Indians?"

"Utes," Eli said, shooting a glance at Joe Moss. "I believe they were Utes. They came in the night and attacked our camp. My poor brother . . ."

Eli sobbed, and it was clear that he wasn't faking his emotions. "Poor Dalton fought like a wild man, but they killed him anyway."

"But you somehow managed to get away."

"I did, barely," Eli said, wiping the tears from his bloodshot eyes with the back of his ragged sleeve. "But my brother is dead! I saw him go down and they swarmed all over him like locusts. Dalton never had a chance. I killed a couple of 'em but there were way too many for me, so I had no choice but to run for my life."

"Damn!" Holt said. "Why didn't you continue on to Placerville and use my money to buy supplies?"

Eli shook his head and carefully considered his answer. "The Utes were still after me. I'd managed to grab this black

gelding, but he ain't fast. If it hadn't been for the night bein'
so dark, those Utes would surely have overtaken and scalped
me."

Holt stared at the two hundred dollars in his big hand as
he considered this setback. Finally, he shrugged and said,
"Well, I'm sorry about Dalton. But we've got the two extra
horses that belonged to Jedediah and Ike. We'll just have to
pack up our stuff and get a move on, although I'm tempted
to go back to Placerville. Maybe we'd find those murderin'
Utes and you could get some payback, Eli."

"Well, sir, I'd like nothin' better, but it's a long ride in
the wrong direction. Those Utes might have followed me
and they could be comin' to kill us like they killed Dalton."

"If they do, it will be the last mistake they ever make,"
Holt said, not seeming a bit worried. "But no matter. We'll
find a little settlement somewhere up ahead in the next few
days, and then we can buy what we need before trying to
get across the Great Basin Desert."

Fiona took a step forward. "You aren't expecting my
Joe to ride a horse now, are you?"

"He either does that or he walks," Holt coldly answered.
"Either way, it's his choice."

"I can ride," Joe decided.

"Yeah, Joe, that's exactly what I thought you'd say,"
Holt told him dismissively.

Fiona looked at Joe and then back at Holt with anxiety
written all over her face. "Mr. Holt, my husband's wounds
are fresh and he's lost a lot of blood. If his horse stumbled
and fell . . ."

"That's the chance he'll have to take," Holt said. "Isn't
that right, Joe?"

"I'll be fine, Fiona," Joe vowed. "I'll get stronger every
day and I can make it."

"See?" Holt told everyone. "This is Joe Moss, better

known among the heathen savages as Man Killer. He's not going to die or quit on us in the desert. He's going to live and try to figure out some way to kill me and Eli so he and his beloved wife can escape a hangman's noose in Virginia City."

"But how are we going to ride horses if we're shackled hand and foot?" Fiona demanded to know.

"Good question," Holt said. "I'll change things around a little so you both can ride. But your feet will be chained under your mounts. That way, if you fall, you won't be leaving your horse."

"We'll be killed," Joe said. "I don't matter much, but Fiona does. Have you ever seen someone tied that way go underneath his horse?"

"No," Holt replied, "I have not. But I can imagine it wouldn't be a pretty sight."

"It isn't," Joe said.

Holt smiled coldly. "I guess that means you and your wife will just have to ride real carefully and not try to escape."

Joe shook his head and then turned to Eli. "I have a question for you."

Eli's head swiveled around suddenly. "I don't have to answer no questions from the likes of you."

Joe shrugged with feigned indifference. "Well, that's true enough, I suppose. But I was just wondering why that black gelding you rode here is shod and has harness marks on his shoulders. That's a plow horse, not an Indian pony you rode in here just now."

Holt looked closer at the horse Eli had ridden in on and then he frowned. "Those are a couple of good questions, Eli. How do you explain the shoes and harness marks?"

"An old mountain man like Moss knows damned good and well that Utes and all other Indians for that matter generally steal their horses from white families."

Eli glared at Joe. "Isn't it a fact that the Utes are especially proud of their horse-stealing ability?"

"It is for a fact," Joe admitted. "But after they steal 'em, they generally don't curry and grain 'em. Looks t' me that the black has been brushed often and grain-fed."

Eli's face darkened. "Moss, are you callin' me a liar?"

"I reckon you're a lot worse'n that," Joe said.

Eli hit Joe with his fist right square in the face. Joe staggered, and would have fallen if Fiona had not grabbed and held him erect.

"Enough!" Holt commanded. "But Joe, just how could you tell if that black has been regularly grained?"

Joe's eyes were locked on Eli, and there was something burning deep in them that made the rifleman swallow hard.

"I asked you a question, Moss. Answer me or when I punch you, that will be all you'll remember until tomorrow."

Joe turned his attention back to Holt. "It's easy to see that the black has been well taken care of and there's more than grass fat on his ribs."

"Well, how about the likelihood that the black was just recently stolen from some Mormon farmer?" Eli demanded. "You ever think of that?"

"I have," Joe said. "And it's possible, but not likely. My money says you're a lyin' sonofabitch, Eli."

Eli balled his fists and started to come at Joe, whose hands were shackled behind his back, but Holt stepped between them. "Eli," he said, "Joe has lost a lot of blood and we need to get him to Virginia City *alive*. Understand?"

"Yeah," Eli said bitterly, "but I am used to killing people who call me a liar."

"You can't kill Joe Moss or touch his wife," Holt ordered. "Because they're like money in our bank. Is that clearly understood?"

"Yeah, I guess."

Holt turned to Joe, and said, "Eli may be a low-down murdering back-shooter, but it was obvious that he and his brother Dalton were close. So let's just put this in the past and get things moving."

"Someday I'll come back here and I'll find those murdering Utes," Eli pledged, rage shaking in his voice. "And I'll kill every last one of them."

"Well," Moss said, "I suppose you can at least try. But that big buffalo rifle that you are so good with? Well, the Utes know exactly how much time it takes to reload, and they'll get your scalp before you could fire a second round. So you might get one Indian down . . . but then they'd be on you like a bird on a bug."

Eli started to say something out of anger, but he checked his words and then headed off to the fire to eat and drink some water before they left this place of death and headed for the Comstock Lode.

✣ 9 ✣

JOE MOSS WAS feeling mighty bad as they rode down into the broken foothills of the Wasatch Range. He had always loved the high green mountains, and even in bad circumstances, mountains had always given him hope and strength. For it was the high mountains that had brought him westward to trap for beaver in the lonely streams, creeks, and rivers. He'd trapped beaver all through the Rockies, then traveled on to the Wasatch, the Big Horns, the Rubys, and even the Cascades up in the Pacific Northwest country. He'd nearly frozen to death dozens of times and he'd faced death on all its cruel terms, and never once had his spirits fallen so low as they were now.

It was Fiona, of course. Joe could stand the thought of his own death because he just figured it was part of the life cycle. He firmly believed, like many of his Indian friends, that there was a Great Spirit and that when a man died, his small spirit lifted out of his body and joined the Great Spirit. And like the Indians of many tribes, he believed that spirits were everywhere and in most everything in this world. All the earth's living animals had spirits, and so, too, did the sky, the earth, and the trees and all the water. To Joe's simple way of thinking, the spirit world that he would one day join had to be a whole lot happier than the earthly world that he'd been struggling through since as long as he could remember.

But dying himself was one thing; allowing Fiona to die was a whole 'nother thing entirely. And if they both swung from a hangman's noose as Holt kept saying, then their little girl, Jessica, would never learn a thing about either of them from the nuns who were taking care of her right now. And sure, Joe knew there were a lot of things about himself and Fiona that their daughter ought not to know, but there were things that he had hoped they could pass on to their child. Fiona, despite all the bad things she'd suffered, was still a fine, brave woman. He'd never had the time to really talk to her about what she thought about Heaven and Hell, but he suspected his wife believed strongly in God, Jesus, and the Holy Bible. That was fine with Joe; their child needed that kind of teaching, which he couldn't give her. But dammit, he could teach her plenty about nature and the outdoors, and even about the Indians and their way of sizin' up the world. He would even teach her how to shoot so that she would be able to protect herself in an emergency . . . or when he grew old, too weak to fight, and died.

Yes, Joe thought as they faced out onto the Great Salt Lake and the vast, shimmering deserts beyond, he could teach little Jessica many, many things and so could his poor wife.

If they survived.

"There it is," Holt said, drawing up his reins and letting his horse stand. "The Great Salt Lake. We'll round it on the north, then hit the desert and head straight southwest toward the Humboldt River." He looked over at Joe. "Did you ever follow that desert basin river?"

"Just once, and that was enough," Joe replied. "It tastes like piss and there ain't no beaver there and probably never was. It's the sorriest excuse for a river I ever saw."

"I've never followed it even once," Holt confessed, "but I've heard from plenty of men that have. They all agree it's the worst river in the West. It tastes alkali, and you have to fear quicksand, with poison snakes and scorpions thick all along its banks. Most of the river's cottonwood trees are long gone, chopped down by the wagon trains for firewood and new axles."

"The Humboldt is a pisser," Joe agreed. "But it's the only water all the way across the desert nearly to Lake Crossin' and the Sierras."

"How far from where the Humboldt vanishes into the sand is it to the Sierras and good water?" Eli asked.

"About sixty miles," Joe reckoned. "Sixty miles of death for wagon trains, whose stock is already thin, weak, and played out. That last sixty miles across the sand with no water is filled with broken wagons, skeletons, and all sorts of treasures that folks had to throw overboard trying to make it out of the desert alive."

"But at least when you get that far, you don't have to worry about the damned Paiutes anymore," Eli said.

"Is that true, Joe?" Holt asked.

"Nope. The Paiutes will jump and kill you right up to Lake Crossin', or Reno, as they're startin' to call it. For that matter, the Paiutes have killed miners workin' just off the Comstock Lode when they think they can get away with it."

"That's also what I've heard," Holt said, making it plain that Joe's word and knowledge were far more valuable than Eli's. "And that's why I think we need to get plenty of supplies and ammunition somewhere down below. I might even hire another man or two to go the distance to the Comstock."

"To hell with that!" Eli exploded. "I figure that I'll be gettin' Dalton's one thousand dollars as well as my own thousand, and I damn sure ain't about to split it up with some new sonsabitches you hire."

"Oh, you'll get what's coming to you, Eli. Don't worry for a single second about that!"

Eli licked his lips and his right hand inched closer to the gun on his hip. "Now, Mr. Holt, I sure do hope you don't have any bad plans in mind for me. Because if you do, we might just as well settle things right here and now between us."

Holt didn't seem the least bit intimidated. "Eli," he said with smooth assurance, "you lost your brother fighting to get a buckboard and supplies that I want and need. You lost Dalton, and then you were honest and forthright enough to return to me with every last dollar of my supply money. That tells me that you are an honorable and brave man."

Holt paused and let his compliments sink in, and saw a smile on Eli's face start to grow. "Now, Eli, why in the world . . . given all the dangers we face crossing the desert up ahead . . . would I have any plans to do you wrong?"

His words were spoken with such utter sincerity that even Joe Moss halfway believed the big man.

Eli flushed and stammered, "Sorry to doubt you, Mr. Holt. You'll have to forgive me for speakin' harshly just now. It's just that I sure do miss my kid brother."

Holt was a model of sympathy. "Of course you do! He was the only family you had in this world. Right?"

"That's right, Mr. Holt. My folks both died of dysentery and I raised little Dalton myself. Protected him until he was strong and fast enough to protect himself." Eli choked with emotion. "I . . . I taught Dalton everything he ever knew and then he got himself killed."

"I'm very, very sorry," Holt said. "Truly I am, and you

will most certainly get not only your promised one thousand dollars, but also that which would have gone to poor Dalton."

"It's only right I do," Eli agreed, his voice choked with gratitude.

"Of course it is!" Holt pointed out toward the vast lake and desert. "Can you see that little settlement way out yonder near the salt lake?"

"I certainly do," Eli replied.

"Well, I'll just bet we can buy a buckboard, water barrels, grain, ammunition, and all our supplies right there before we leave the good water and strike out for the bad."

Eli's voice took on a pleading tone. "I *sure* could use some whiskey, Mr. Holt. A bottle of whiskey and a good drunk would help me deal with losin' poor Dalton. Most certainly it would!"

"Then you shall have a bottle of the best that can be found!"

Eli brightened up, and so did Joe Moss. If Eli got roaring drunk, that meant he would be worthless and make it easier for Joe and Fiona to make their escape.

"What about you, Joe Moss?" Holt asked.

"What about me?" Joe asked suspiciously.

"Would you like a little red-eye?"

"I never turned whiskey down, good nor bad."

"Well, I'm not an entirely unkind man. If you and your woman will promise me no grief, I might even see if we can find a doctor to examine that shoulder wound."

"Fiona has tended it well and it's on the mend," Joe replied.

"Maybe Fiona needs some medicines and even . . . a bath and a clean dress."

Fiona's eyes widened with surprise and something almost akin to hope. Joe was glad to see both, but he didn't trust Ransom Holt as far as he could have thrown the giant with one arm. And promising them whiskey, a bath, and a new dress for Fiona? Well, that would happen the day that fat pigs flew over the moon.

"Would you like a bath and a new dress?" Holt asked.

Before she could answer, Joe snapped, "Don't be makin' promises to my good wife, Mr. Holt. The only promises to be made to her will come from *me*."

Holt laughed with derision. "Why, Joe Moss, the only thing that you can promise her is more suffering, and after that the hard hemp of a noose around her skinny neck! So why shouldn't she have something nice before she hangs?"

Fiona lifted her chin. "I don't want anything from you, sir!"

"Of course you do. And to be honest, I don't want to drag you into Virginia City looking dirty and nearly dead. Those Comstock miners will expect to see a white woman hang who actually looks like a white woman. A pretty white woman will bring a big, paying crowd. A poor, skinny wretch like you won't bring much of a crowd, and may even earn some sympathy, which is definitely not what Peabody wants."

"I get it," Joe said. "You want Fiona lookin' clean and pretty so the crowd will be bigger and pay more to watch."

"Yes," Holt said. "That's the way it was explained to me by Mr. Peabody, and I certainly do see his point. That's the reason, Mrs. Moss, why your life is going to improve somewhat. A new dress or two before we get to Virginia City. Maybe even a comb for your hair, which is now so tangled and filthy that I find it repulsive."

"Find it what?" Joe asked, not knowing the meaning of that word.

"Repulsive. Disgusting. Joe, your wife's red hair looks like the red ass end of a sick fox," Holt explained. "It needs to be washed and then brushed to a shine. Didn't she have beautiful, shining hair when you first met her?"

"Well, yeah, she did," Joe said, "but—"

"But nothing," Holt interrupted. "Although she looks like hell right now, I expect that she was once quite striking. And why shouldn't you want her to look nice again?"

"Because she don't need anything from you," Joe said.

"Well, I think you're wrong to feel that way. What about you, Fiona? Wouldn't you like a bath and a clean dress? Maybe a comb for your hair and even shoes to cover your poor feet?"

Joe glanced at his wife, waiting for her to tell Holt that he could just go straight to hell. But instead, Fiona managed a smile and said, "I'd like that very much. If I have to die, I want to die looking my best."

"Ha!" Holt barked. "Even after all that you've suffered, you still retain some pride and even vanity."

"I do," she said, avoiding Joe's hard glare of disapproval.

Holt was pleased. "Well, then, we shall see what we can do for you down in that settlement before we start across the desert."

Joe started to say something, but Fiona's glance told him to shut up and that she would explain her words and actions later. He sure hoped so. If she was beginning to soften up and think of Ransom Holt as a decent, caring human being, then they were as good as already hanged.

✤ 10 ✤

THE AIR GREW very warm and windy when they came
down off the mountains and started around the north
end of the Great Salt Lake. Out around the lake, they saw
towering white dust devils spinning and dancing through
the stunted sage and vultures soaring on the rising hot-air
currents. Now, instead of pines as far westward as a man
could see, there was just an ocean of stunted brush and yel-
lowed grasses. The lake itself shimmered in the afternoon
sunlight, and seagulls squawked and soared over the water
or walked along the salty shore looking for dead fish.

The town of Perdition was strung along the banks of a
clear creek that fed out of the mountains and ran down into
the alkali and salt flats. A big sign at the eastern edge of the
settlement warned travelers that this was the last chance for
them to trade lame horses for sound ones or take on fresh
provisions for the brutal push westward toward the Humboldt River.

"Everything in Perdition will cost about double what
you'd expect to pay," Joe Moss observed as they rode into

the bleak, sun-hammered town. "This is a rough Mormon settlement and the people who live here are considered to be religious outcasts. Sinners of the worst sort . . . which is why I always liked to come through Perdition."

"Moss, what do you mean?" Holt demanded.

"It means that no one who lives in Perdition is held in high favor by Brigham Young or his powerful church friends. They're all 'Jack Mormons' who don't follow their church's rules to the letter. And besides that, maybe these people just were too lazy to be good Mormon farmers. But for whatever the reason, the people who live in Perdition were sent out here where the ground is poor and salt and alkali dust burns your skin and your eyes. These people smoke and drink rotgut whiskey, but not openly because they're livin' too close to Salt Lake City. There are whores and gambling in Perdition, none of which is out in the open."

"These people sound like a bunch of misfits to me," Holt said, not bothering to lower his voice.

"You could call 'em that," Joe agreed. "But they're rebels and I like their independent spirit."

"Why don't they all just move away?" Holt asked. "I don't see a damn thing about this land or settlement that would encourage anyone to stay."

"They're all sharp traders," Joe told the man. "Some of 'em are almost rich, as a matter of fact, and gettin' richer every time a wagon train or some ignorant pilgrims come through here desperate for supplies or fresh horses. Also, the men of Perdition are tough and depended upon by Brigham Young to keep the Paiutes at bay."

"You're saying they protect Salt Lake City from Indian raids?"

"No," Joe said, "that's not what I'm exactly sayin'. But let's say, for example, that some Paiutes get drunk and take it upon themselves to raid a farm down in the good part of the valley. Well, rather than send hardworking, God-fearin' farmers after the Paiutes, they send the men from Perdition to do the dirty work. There are men here who can shoot almost as well as myself and who aren't afraid of anything."

"Sounds like I'd best be on my guard," Ransom Holt said more to himself than to Joe. "But it also sounds like I ought to be able to find a man or two here that would help us get safely across the desert to Reno."

"Just remember," Eli said, "what wages you pay any new men ain't comin' out of my share or that of my dead brother."

"I'll remember," Holt snapped. "And if you want me to pay for your drunk, you'd damn sure better mind your manners."

"Sorry, boss."

"Eli, stick close until we got a place to spend the night and we've got our prisoners well secured. After that, we'll buy what we need and then you can go on your drunk. But you'd better be ready to leave tomorrow morning at first light. I don't like the looks of Perdition. No, sir! Not one little bit do I like the looks of what I'm seeing."

Joe understood the giant's feelings. As they rode into the settlement, it seemed like everyone in this run-down, hard-looking town came out to give them the once-over with cold, appraising eyes. From the lean, dirty men to the skinny dirty women and children of Perdition, they all had a predatory look, and not one waved in greeting or offered so much as a hello or a smile.

"This place gives me a *real* bad feeling," Eli told his boss. "I'm not sure that I want to get dead drunk here tonight. If I did, I might get murdered and robbed."

"You might at that," Holt agreed.

"Maybe I'll take that bottle of whiskey you promised

and get blind drunk tomorrow night when we're camped out in the sagebrush north of the lake."

"That would probably be a smart thing to do," Holt said. "Wouldn't you agree, Joe?"

"I don't give a damn when or where Eli gets drunk. And as far as gettin' himself killed, it might as well be today, for it's sure comin' tomorrow."

"You just try to kill me, you sonofabitch!" Eli snarled.

Fiona stared at a slovenly woman with a big goiter on her neck and no teeth in her mouth. The woman probably wasn't any older than herself, and she looked mean, jaded, and cruel. "Mr. Holt," Fiona said, "I feel like Eli about Perdition and I'd just as soon get that bath, dress, and comb later. These people look like they hate us on sight."

"They probably do," Holt said. "All right, it's decided. I'll buy what we must have here, and then we'll get out of Perdition before the sun goes down. But I'm still looking for a man or two . . . the kind that can shoot straight and who won't cut and run if we get into trouble."

Joe frowned and said, "There are three liveries in Perdition. I'd recommend you deal with an old one-legged man who owns the last livery right at the edge of the desert."

"What's his name?"

"Micah," Joe said.

"And this Micah is honest?" Holt asked.

"I didn't say that."

"Well, then . . ."

"Ain't nobody honest in Perdition," Joe explained. "But Micah is less dishonest than most."

"What about the supplies we need for the desert crossing?"

Joe pointed to a log cabin where a bunch of mongrels were lounging around in the afternoon shade. "That'd be my choice."

"All right," Holt said. "We'll get a buckboard and a team of horses at the livery, and then drive 'em back to that log cabin and get whatever supplies we have to have before we head out into the desert."

"What about us?" Joe said. "Are we supposed to sit on our horses in the sun chained together like slaves?"

Holt swiveled around in his saddle and studied the town and its hard-eyed inhabitants. "That's the way it'll have to be, Joe," he finally decided. "I'm thinking that a man as bad as you might just have some good friends in Perdition. If that is the case, I want them to see that you are my prisoner and that I'm not a man to be crossed."

"I can handle anything you can dish out," Joe said, "but Fiona is a woman and it's too hard on her to sit her horse for hours in chains right out in this damned hot sun."

Holt gave that a moment's thought. "All right. Eli, you lead our prisoners and their horses over to that big tree and unchain their feet. Let them dismount and rest in the shade."

"That's the best that you're going to do for us here?" Fiona asked, voice filled with anger. "We haven't eaten since yesterday and I need to do my business in private."

"Lift your dirty skirt and do your business behind that big tree," Holt ordered before riding off to the livery to buy a wagon and horses.

When Holt rode up to the livery, sure enough an old, one-legged man came out of his barn with straw stuck to his breeches. The liveryman was small, thin, and not a bit friendly. He asked, "What do you need, big man?"

"I need a buckboard and a team of horses. Five or six hundred pounds of grain, a few extra ropes, and harness."

"I can provide what you need, big man, providing you got the money to pay."

"Let me see what you have to sell me," Holt said. "And then perhaps we'll talk price."

"You'll like my horses. They're all sound and in good flesh. My name is Micah. I only deal in cash or gold."

"I have federal cash."

"That will do," Micah said. "Come look at the horses and then I'll show you what wagons and harness I have to sell. How about saddles?"

"Don't need any saddles."

"Too bad," Micah told him. "I've got about a dozen and I'd sell the lot of them cheap. Got some Indian ponies, too. But they ain't strong enough to pull a wagon. They're just small, runty mustangs."

"No mustangs," Holt said. "I want big, strong horses or mules."

"What about oxen?"

"Too slow," Holt said.

"Slow but steadier, and they do real well on that sage-brush and salt grass you're gonna see so much of on the way west."

"Maybe," Holt said, "but I don't like oxen, so just show me mules and horses."

Two hours later, Holt drove a buckboard and a team of four good Missouri mules out of the livery and his wallet was $130 lighter. The cost was much higher than it should have been, or would have been in Laramie or even Denver or St. Louis, but Holt understood that he was not in a strong bargaining position, and so he paid without whining. He was going to be short of money for supplies, and that meant that they'd have to do without much whiskey and food, but he'd buy all the extra ammunition that they would require for the desert trek.

Ignoring Joe, Fiona, and Eli, who were resting in the shade of the tree, Ransom Holt drove over to the log cabin that served as a general store. He was about to climb down from the buckboard when two men were knocked backpedaling through the log cabin's open doorway. Their faces were covered with blood and they staggered off the porch, then spilled to the ground.

Holt froze on his wagon seat as a tall young man, a half-breed by the looks of him, stepped out of the log cabin and shouted at the battered pair, "You got anything else to say about my mother and my Cheyenne blood?"

Both of the battered and bloody men on the ground swore and went for the guns on their hips. The half-breed also wore a six-gun, and it came out of his worn holster faster than the blink of a cat's eye. The gun in the breed's hand bucked just twice, and Holt saw crimson roses appear in the center of the two men's chests as if by magic. Drilled through their hearts, both men were dead before their boot heels could drum the alkali dust.

The half-breed holstered his gun and started to step over the bodies and leave.

"Hey!" another voice yelled, and the breed twisted around to see the owner of the general store emerge holding a shotgun aimed at his chest. "Breed, you busted up my place and now you're gonna pay!"

Holt could almost see the half-breed's mind working as his hand strayed toward his holstered pistol. But the shotgun was cocked and there was no way the store owner could have missed blowing the breed all to hell.

After a moment's deliberation, the breed's shoulders sagged and he raised his hands shoulder high. "You got the drop on me, mister. But I didn't start that fight in your store. Those two did, and so they're the ones that owe you for damages, not me."

"Well, you killed 'em so now they *can't* pay me! And

since you finished the fight in a permanent way, are you gonna pay for what you destroyed, or shall I just put you down right now with those other two?"

"I ain't got but two bits," the half-breed said, his dark eyes showing no fear as he looked up at the furious store owner. "But, mister, you could take the guns and boots off those dead men and that surely would be enough to pay for all your damages."

"Yeah," the store owner said, "but just to make sure, I could kill you and have three guns, two pair of boots, and those fancy beaded Injun moccasins that you're wearing. How's that sound? Huh, breed?"

"Sounds like you mean to kill me no matter what," the breed replied. "I got cash money to pay, so why don't you put that shotgun down?"

"Let's see your money, breed! And keep your hand away from that gun. I saw how fast you drew and fired on those two."

"Yes, sir," the breed said quietly. "My money is tucked into my money belt just behind my backbone."

"Let's see it!"

Holt watched the half-breed reach behind his back, and instead of finding a money belt, he found a large hunting knife. The knife came out faster than the strike of a snake, and the breed hurled it with tremendous accuracy and force, then threw himself sideways as the shotgun exploded harmlessly into the sky.

The hunting knife had found its mark.

The storekeeper dropped his empty shotgun and stared down at the deer-antler handle of the hunting knife protruding from his belly. After a moment, he slowly looked up with shock and amazement at the half-breed. "You . . . you stinkin' red breed bastard!" the store owner choked out before he toppled off his porch to land beside the other two dead men.

The half-breed snatched his gun out of his holster and spun around to cover Ransom Holt, who was the only man close enough to have witnessed the sudden deaths. "You want any of this, big man?"

"Hell, no," Ransom said, throwing up both of his huge hands. "I'm out of it!"

"Smart man."

The half-breed quickly rummaged through the pockets of the three bodies, pulling out cash, and then he jammed their pistols under his gun belt and snatched up the store owner's fine shotgun.

"Big man, tell these Mormon assholes that if they come after me, a lot more white-eyes will die before the sun goes down!"

"I'll tell them," Holt promised.

The breed shook his head and his long, black hair waved. "And . . . and tell them it was self-defense. You saw it, mister! I *had* to kill them all or they'd have killed me."

"I'll tell them exactly what I saw. It was self-defense and there is no question about it."

"Sure it was . . . but you're one of them, so I expect they'll try to track me down and kill me," the half-breed hissed a moment before he took off running down the street headed west into the desert.

Within five minutes, most of the population of Perdition was standing around the three dead men and Holt was retelling for the third time how the half-breed had been forced to kill these men in self-defense.

"I had already paid the store owner for supplies and was coming back to pick them up with this wagon I just bought from Micah," Ransom smoothly lied. "And now, if you people don't mind, I'm going to collect the supplies that I paid for and leave this godforsaken town of Perdition."

There was some arguing that maybe Holt was not telling the whole truth, but when Holt turned his hard eyes on those who spoke such foolish words, that kind of talk fell silent.

Holt marched into the general store like he had bought the whole place, and quickly filled three feed sacks of supplies including five boxes of ammunition. He would have emptied the cash drawer, too, if there hadn't been sullen townsmen watching his every move.

"So long," Holt said to no one in particular.

A thin, pocked-faced man blocked his path and demanded, "Stranger, how do we know you paid for all those goods?"

Holt knew you could never run just a half bluff, so he leaned over the man and hissed, "You're just gonna have to take my word for it or else call me a liar, and then Perdition will have *four* gawddamn Mormon funerals in one day. Which is it to be, mister?"

The pocked-faced man looked into Holt's black, pitiless eyes and nervously licked his thin lips, saying, "No offense, stranger. Come to think of it, I reckon you're tellin' the truth after all."

"I reckon I am," Holt growled as he bulled his way past the men while hauling his three heavy feed sacks of supplies over his shoulder. He swung the sacks up into the buckboard, climbed into the wagon, and took a second to study the dead men.

Holt raised his eyes to the sullen, suspicious crowd and hollered, "If I were you folks, I'd not try to go after the half-breed kid. I'm the only witness and I tell you it was a case of self-defense."

"But he's a damn Cheyenne!" someone swore.

"Half Cheyenne," Holt corrected. "And I say one more time that he's innocent of all these deaths."

"Who the hell are *you*?" someone from the angry-faced crowd demanded.

Holt sought out the speaker and replied, "I'm the man who is just about damn good and ready to jump down from this buckboard and kick your ass up between your shoulder blades!"

The man shut up and the crowd parted as Holt drove his wagon and his supplies over to the big tree where Eli was guarding Joe and Fiona Moss.

"Did you see what happened just now in front of the log cabin?" Holt asked.

"I seen it," Eli said with wonder in his voice. "But then I swear, it's hard for me to believe what I actually did see. That half-breed has the fastest hands I ever saw in my life. Faster than poor Dalton's hands even."

"Joe Moss, did you see those three killings?" Holt asked.

"I saw them, and the half-breed was only trying to save his life. He didn't want to kill the store owner, and he wouldn't have done it 'cept he could see that the fool was going to blow a hole through him."

"Yeah, that's the way I saw it, too," Holt agreed. "Self-defense in all three cases. That half-breed is a born killer as gawd is my witness."

Eli said, "That half-breed was not only fast with a gun and a knife—he was fast on his feet. Why, he flew down this street past us and out into the desert like he had wings on his moccasins."

"When I was his age, I could run like that one," Joe said to himself. "But he's fast. Real fast."

"Let's get out of here while the crowd is still fascinated with the three dead men," Holt suggested.

"Did you buy all the supplies we need?" Eli asked.

"I didn't buy anything," Holt said with a smirk and a wink. "But how could any of those Jack Mormons know that I was lying?"

"You mean that you just went in and filled those three sacks for free?" Eli asked with admiration filling his voice.

"That's right. Why should you pay for something when you can have it for nothing?"

Eli helped Fiona up onto her little sorrel mare, and then chained her ankles together under the horse before he did the same thing to Joe Moss.

"Fiona, I got you a couple of dresses," said Holt. "There was no time to look at the sizes, so they're probably going to be too big."

"Any whiskey?" Eli asked.

"Naw," Holt said, "I was moving too fast and it must have been hidden somewhere."

"Damn," Eli swore.

"We'll find us some on the road to Reno," Holt promised. "Now let's get out of this town," he ordered, slapping a whip over his new team of Missouri mules and hurrying west out of Perdition.

"HEY, BOSS, IT'S gettin' pretty dark," Eli called. "Don't you think we should pull up and make camp?"

"Let's try to push it a couple of more miles," Holt said. "I want to get as much distance between ourselves and Perdition as we can this evening."

Eli grumbled, "But in the dark we could drive that buckboard into a pothole or deep rut and bust a wagon wheel. Or there could be Paiutes skulkin' around out here in the brush! Hellfire, if we keep movin' in the dark, we're just askin' for trouble."

"All right, another mile," Holt said, not wanting to cave in to the man's sound logic. "Another mile and then we'll make camp. But no fire! Not tonight anyway."

"You think we've got enough barrels filled with water to get all the way to the Humboldt River?" Eli asked. "Five barrels don't seem like that much to me, given us and all the livestock we've got."

"Micah said five barrels would get us all the way to a place called Salt Springs."

"Salt Springs! Shit! That doesn't sound like good water to me!" Eli complained.

"Shut up and let's keep movin'."

Joe and Fiona were once more shackled by the ankles with chains running under the bellies of their horses. And their horses were now securely halter-tied to the back of the buckboard that Ransom Holt was driving. Joe's spirits were even lower than they had been the day before entering Perdition. Now it seemed like they were in even tougher circumstances. And if Eli's worst fears materialized and they were jumped by Paiutes, well, Joe and Fiona were as good as butchered beef.

"All right," Holt called after they'd plodded along for another hour. "Let's pull up here and make camp."

"It ain't much of a place to camp, Mr. Holt. Right here in the middle of the road with sagebrush crowdin' us."

"It will do," Holt said, sounding testy. "Eli, just quit your bitchin' and unsaddle the horses and unhitch the mules. Make sure that you tie them to the wagon and grain them at least a pound apiece. And give them a full bucket of water apiece, too."

"How come I got to do all the work?" Eli groused. "What are you gonna do, Mr. Holt?"

"I'm going to rest and keep watch over Joe and Fiona until about three in the morning, at which time I'll wake your lazy ass and you'll keep watch over them until dawn."

"Damn, how come we gotta do that?"

"Because those Paiutes you worry about so much would love to catch us all sleeping. Isn't that right, Joe?"

"I reckon so," Joe said.

"And you'd be as helpless as a kitten if the Paiutes came

to lift your scalp," Holt said with a yawn as he unshackled Joe and Fiona and then watched them dismount before he reshackled them again to the wagon. "I got some sourdough bread and salt pork. We'll eat and then sleep."

"How do we sleep standing up?" Fiona asked with unconcealed sarcasm.

"I'll chain you to opposite sides of the wagon on the wheels," Holt decided. "Now let's just get settled in and everybody shut the hell up. It's been a long day . . . but a profitable one."

"I'm still thinkin' about that half-breed and how he could draw that pistol and fire, and then how he throw'd that big hunting knife and got the storekeeper right in the guts," Eli said as he unhitched the mules. "That fella was somethin' to watch!"

"He took off running this way," Holt told the man. "So that's another reason why we have to keep a watch out all night."

"I don't think he would have anything to do with us," Eli said, his voice lacking conviction. "I mean, that Cheyenne Injun kid was just trying to save his own neck."

"Yeah," Holt agreed. "And he might just decide to kill us and steal everything."

"Maybe you're right at that," Eli said. "We'll have to watch out for that one."

It was almost dawn when the young half-breed who called himself Johnny Redman crept up on the sleeping camp of whites. He had watched the giant hand over the guard to the one with the Sharps rifle, and then within an hour, they were both sound asleep.

Johnny needed a horse, and several horses would be even better. And he would like to have the Sharps rifle that was leaning up beside the wagon. For that matter, he'd like to steal the buckboard, mules, and all those supplies. And the barrels of water would take him all the way across the deserts, if he was able to find the Paiute water holes that few people except Indians knew about.

Now, with the first gray light of a new day creeping up on the eastern horizon, Johnny Redman moved into the camp on moccasins that allowed him to step as silent as a ghost. One of the horses jerked its head around to watch Johnny, but then it lost interest. Fortunately, these people had no dogs.

Redman slipped into camp and took the Sharps rifle, and then he went to the horses and mules and began to untie them one by one. He was doing just fine when a low voice said, "If you steal our livestock, we'll have to hunt you down and kill you."

Redman whirled and faced the tall man chained to the wagon wheel. "Oh, it's just you," he said. "You're not like the giant and the other one."

"No," Joe Moss said, keeping his voice real quiet. "I'm not."

"I could kill you easy," Johnny declared.

"Not before I shouted and woke up Ransom Holt and Eli. And they won't be as easy to kill as those you put down back in Perdition."

Redman considered this. "What do you want?"

Joe didn't have to think twice before answering. "I want to be free. The key to the locks are in the big man's pants pocket."

"I can't get those keys without waking him."

"Then kill him and take the keys," Joe said.

"Uh-uh," Johnny Redman said. "I don't kill sleeping people unless they are my enemy. And I don't know that big man or the other one you call Eli."

"They are my enemies," Joe explained. "And I will pay you well to kill them."

"No," the half-breed decided after a moment of consideration. "But if you yell, then I will kill you quick."

Joe knew the half-breed would do exactly as he said and that there sure wasn't much point in dying for giving Holt and Eli a warning. "All right, I won't yell. But I saw you take guns from those two dead men. How about giving me one of those guns?"

"I can't do that."

"Why not?"

"Because you might decide to shoot me."

"Hmmm," Joe said. "I ain't seein' myself gettin' anything for keepin' quiet and lettin' you steal our livestock."

"You get to keep your life," Johnny told him. "And that's plenty good enough."

Joe nodded in silent resignation, then whispered, "They're takin' me and my wife, Fiona, to Virginia City for a bounty of at least three thousand dollars."

Johnny stopped what he was doing. "Three thousand dollars!"

"Yep."

Johnny grinned. "You must have done something very bad for them to pay that much for your necks."

"I killed some rich mine owners in a place called Gold Hill right next to Virginia City. They were brothers and the last one alive is willin' to pay most anything to have me hang before a Comstock crowd."

"Why are you telling me this now and why should I even care?"

"Because the big man badly needs help getting us across this desert alive," Joe whispered. "And I don't think we have much of a chance without some help."

"And?" Johnny asked.

"Why steal a few guns and horses worth so little when you could get a thousand dollars for helping the big man deliver us and collect a bounty on the Comstock Lode?"

"Would he pay me well to help?"

"Sure as hell he would," Joe told the young half-breed. "But I have to tell you that I mean to get free and kill that pair. Maybe, if you treated my woman kindly, I would let you keep your half-breed Cheyenne scalp."

Johnny Redman leaned forward so that his face was only inches from that of Joe Moss. "You are a mountain man and the one that my people call Man Killer."

"That's right. How did you know that?"

"I know many things, Man Killer. And I know that my people always trusted you to keep your word. So I believe it when you say that there is a big reward for you and your woman."

"And you can have some of it if you can figure a way to get us to the Comstock alive," Joe offered.

"But would you also kill me to escape?"

"Yes," Joe said, knowing that this half-breed would sense a lie.

Johnny Redman leaned back and frowned with concentration. Finally, he asked, "What do I have to do to get the big man to hire me for this journey?"

"Well," Joe said, "if I were you, I'd start by putting the Sharps rifle back where you found it and then the horses and mules. Put everything back and disappear into the brush. Come morning, I'll tell Ransom Holt that you paid us a little visit just before daylight."

"And what would he say to that?"

"He will be very angry with Eli for falling asleep on guard, but his anger will cool quickly when I tell him that you want to help him get us to Virginia City."

"How far away is this place?"

"Five hundred miles. Maybe a little more."

"And if you tell him I want one thousand dollars of bounty money, then what will the big man say?"

"He will say yes," Joe replied, "but the other one will get very angry and threaten to fight."

"So will they fight?"

"No," Joe Moss said. "Eli will back down, but he will wait for a chance to kill the big man and then kill me and my wife for *all* the bounty."

"Man Killer, I could kill him right now and take his place," Johnny Redman reasoned.

"We need him," Joe said. "Eli is a marksman and he will not run if we are jumped by Paiutes. I have no doubt that he is a good and fierce fighter."

"Even if he is afraid of the big man?"

"Even so," Joe told the half-breed.

Johnny Redman replaced the big rifle. He returned everything to its place, and then he crept back to Joe Moss just as the sun slipped over the far eastern horizon. "I will be up ahead, Man Killer. You tell the big man that Johnny Redman was here and did not kill him or the rest of you because he wants one thousand dollars of the reward."

"I will tell him that," Joe promised. "And tonight when the sun is low and we make camp, come to join us."

"I will be ready to kill them if they try to kill me," the half-breed warned.

"I would like that," Joe said. "If you want to try and kill them both, that would help me and Fiona."

"But then I would not get the reward."

"No," Joe said, "you would not."

"I will go now and think about these things that we have spoken about," Johnny Redman said.

"With a thousand dollars, you could do anything you wanted to do," Joe told the half-breed as he was leaving.

"Yes, but you and your woman would hang."

"Yes," Joe admitted, "we would have to hang and I do not mean for that to happen."

"I do not want you as my enemy," Johnny Redman said. "I have always heard my people speak well of you."

"Was it your mother . . . or your father that was Cheyenne?"

"My father. He took my white mother on a raid and she became like a Cheyenne. The soldiers killed them both when I was twelve years old. I was taken in by other families, and then I left my Cheyenne people looking for something I have not yet found."

"What would that be?"

"Revenge against all the soldiers."

"Revenge is good sometimes," Joe told the half-breed, "but it is like a thirst that can never be satisfied. And one day, it will kill your body and even your soul."

"So I have been told by the wisest among my people. Man Killer, I will give these things we have talked about much thought today," Johnny Redman promised as he vanished like a wraith into the cool desert dawn.

✦ 12 ✦

SOMEHOW, ELI MANAGED to wake up a few minutes before Ransom Holt the next morning, so he avoided catching hell. Just after dawn, Joe and Fiona rode out of the camp shackled on horseback, even though Fiona had pleaded that Joe be allowed to stretch out on blankets in the buckboard.

"To hell with that," Holt snapped. "Joe could get loose and then strangle me from behind while I'm driving. I like the way things are now, so we'll stay this way clear to the Comstock."

"If we're attacked by Paiutes," Joe warned, "our situation could get ugly real fast. I'd be a lot more useful to you in the buckboard than shackled to this horse."

"I'll take my chances with the Paiutes over you any day of the week," Holt told him.

Eli snickered. "Joe, I'll take my chances with that wife of yours if you get scalped by Paiutes."

Joe bristled and bit back a response. Sooner or later he would have Eli's hair, and then they'd see who had the last laugh.

"What's the matter, Joe Moss? Cat got your tongue?" Eli said, trying to goad him into a response.

"How'd you sleep last night, Eli?" Joe decided to ask.

"I slept well until three o'clock this morning when I went on guard."

"You slept well even after that," Joe said loud enough for Ransom Holt to overhear. "In fact, Eli, you slept so well that you didn't even know we had a visitor."

"What are you talking about?" Holt demanded.

"I'm just saying that we were paid a visit last night by that Cheyenne half-breed kid that killed those three men in Perdition."

"What!" Holt drew the wagon to a halt. "What did you say?"

"You heard me," Joe replied. "The kid's name is Johnny Redman and he came to steal your mules and horses as well as Eli's Sharps rifle and maybe both your scalps."

Holt's face turned purple with rage. He glared at Eli, who looked away quickly. "Eli, damn your lazy hide, is Moss telling me the truth?"

"No, sir! I never closed my eyes even for a minute between the time that you waked me this mornin' and first light when we all got movin'."

"He's lying to you," Joe said matter-of-factly. "The half-breed kid sneaked into our camp, and would have killed all of you and stolen everything if I hadn't convinced him to pay us a visit tonight."

"Now why would he do that?" Holt asked.

"Because," Joe said, "I told him about the huge bounty that you are planning to get from that Peabody fella."

"You told him that?"

"I did for a fact," Joe said. "And I told him that he'd make a lot more money by helping get us to the Comstock

Lode than he would by killing you two last night in your sleep."

Holt and Eli exchanged glances, then Holt said, "Tell me more about this conversation."

"All right," Joe agreed, "I told Johnny Redman that the reward for getting myself and Fiona to the Comstock Lode was going to be at least three thousand dollars."

"How the hell would you know what the full reward is?" Holt demanded. "I've never told you or anyone else the exact amount."

"I don't for certain," Joe confessed. "But the way that Peabody has been throwin' his money at the spies you hired, and the fact that Eli and Dalton were supposed to get a thousand apiece, tells me that the whole pot has to be at least three thousand . . . and maybe a heap more."

Holt had to smile. "You're a hell of a lot brighter than you look, Moss. But I'm not going to pay that half-breed gunslinger any thousand dollars."

"Suit yourself," Joe said, "but that'll be what he's expecting."

"I'll kill the half-breed for you!" Eli shouted to Holt. "If he shows up at our camp tonight, then I'll just shoot him in the guts and we'll all sit around the campfire and watch him slowly die."

"You can try to kill Johnny Redman," Joe said, "but were I a bettin' man, I'd sure as hell put my money on the half-breed before I'd put it on you."

Eli shook with anger. "Moss," he grated, "I almost wish that Mr. Holt would just take off those chains so that we could fight it out to the death."

"No, you don't," Joe told the man. "Because even with a hole in my shoulder not completely healed, I'd still carve you up like a Christmas turkey and then take your scalp.

Give us both knives or guns, and you wouldn't last any longer than a snowball in hell."

"Maybe we should find out right now!" Eli yelled, jumping off his horse and acting like he was fixing to fight.

"Maybe we shouldn't," Holt said sternly. "Eli, get back on that horse and quit acting like a damned fool. Can't you see that Moss is just trying to goad you into a fight?"

"Well, I'm not backin' away from one!"

"You should be," Holt told his gunman. "Moss would kill you in less than a minute, and then I wouldn't have anyone to help me deliver him and his wife to Peabody. And that's exactly what he wants to happen. Now get back on that horse and stop acting like a damn fool!"

Eli glared at Joe, who simply smiled back at the man. Eli was a fool and sooner or later he would do something rash, and then Joe figured he would have his chance to kill the man.

"So," Holt said as he got the buckboard moving again. "This half-breed is going to show up at our camp tonight and demand a thousand dollars?"

"That's what he said."

"Maybe I should agree to that," Holt mused aloud.

"What?" Eli cried. "I lost my brother and I'm gettin' Dalton's full share. *Me!* Not some half-breed who just showed up yesterday."

"Listen," Holt said, "what I pay is my business. You'll get your two thousand dollars. I've already agreed to that, and so will Peabody when I tell him how you stuck with me right from the start and how it cost you your only brother. Mr. Peabody recently lost two of his brothers . . . thanks to Joe Moss and his wife. So there's no doubt that he will be willing to pay you what I've promised."

The anger seeped out of Eli's face. "It's only right that I

get paid both my share as well as Dalton's. I'd rather have my brother back than the money, you know."

"Is that a fact?" Joe questioned. "I sure don't believe it."

"Gawddamn you!" Eli screamed at Joe. "You keep pushin' me and I'm going to kill you!"

"You do that," Holt said, his voice cold as ice, "and I'll kill *you*."

Eli bit back his anger and spurred his horse on ahead. Holt looked at Joe Moss and said, "You know, Eli is pretty hot-tempered and after losing his brother, he might just go crazy and kill you."

"Yeah, he might," Joe told the big man, "but then again, he might just get himself killed in the process."

"So then you and Eli would both be dead and I'd only have your wife to take on to the Comstock Lode for a hanging. Is that how you want this game to play out, Moss?"

Joe had to finally shake his head. "No," he admitted. "That's not what I want."

"Then you had better stop needling Eli," Holt warned. "For your own good as well as mine."

"He's not going to make it all the way to the Comstock Lode," Joe said. "We both know you'll kill him before you have to pay him."

"You don't know a gawddamn thing! Now shut your mouth or I won't give your wife any water when we stop to rest at noon."

"You're a hard, hard man," Joe said between clenched teeth.

"So are you," Holt told him as they drove on. "And I'll tell you one other thing as long as we're on the subject."

"What is that?"

"I don't think it's going to work out with the half-breed hiring on to help me get you to Virginia City."

"Why not?"

"Because he's too damn fast with a gun or a knife," Holt reasoned. "Faster than you and faster than me."

"That's true enough," Joe said. "But this country is full of Paiutes. They've been at war with the whites since the first wagon trains started coming through cutting down all the trees along the Humboldt River. Just as bad, the emigrants have been cutting down for firewood the piñon pines, which give those Indians piñon nuts, their main source of food. The whites have shot out whatever deer that used to run wild in this desert, they've polluted the springs and water holes, and they've hunted the wild mustangs just for sport."

"So," Holt said with amusement. "The emigrants have basically screwed up everything for the Paiutes. Is that what you're trying to tell me?"

"I'm not trying to tell you anything," Joe said. "I've just explained why the Paiutes hate all the whites. And when they see that we're all by ourselves with just one wagon and two men able to fight, you can be sure that they'll come against us."

"How?"

"You're asking me how to guard against the Paiutes?" Joe asked.

"That's right," Holt replied. "I'm asking you how we can best protect ourselves. And you're telling me, unless you want your wife to not only go without water but without food today."

"You ornery sonofabitch!" Joe whispered. "You're gonna use Fiona against me every step of the way, aren't you?"

"That's right," Holt said pleasantly. "So you might just as well cooperate and help me all that you can."

Joe scowled. "All right," he conceded. "The Paiute are a desert people and they're as good at tracking and stalking in this rough desert country as the Apache. And like the Apache, they won't attack us on horseback. No, sir. They'll sneak up in this sagebrush and they'll try to ambush both you and Eli."

"So how do we stop them from doing that?" Holt asked with real concern in his voice.

"Best way is to have an outrider who knows how to look for Indians and their signs. That's why we need to hire Johnny Redman. He can ride out in front and give us some advance warning. Otherwise, we're just riding into a Paiute death trap. It ain't a matter of if . . . it's a matter of when and where."

"So you say," Holt told him. "Yet this is mighty big country with damn little feed or water. What makes you so sure that the Paiute will even see us as we pass through their desert?"

"Well," Joe reasoned, "if *you* were a white-man-hatin' Indian, wouldn't you just naturally stick around the only road through this desert and be on the watch for anyone following the Humboldt River?"

Holt grudgingly nodded his head with understanding. "Yes," he said, "if I were a Paiute wanting to kill or rob whites, then I would watch this road and the river trail."

"So there you have it," Joe told the man. "The Paiute won't let anyone pass without givin' them a good once-over. And when they see a lone wagon and just a few men, they'll decide it's easy pickin's. And I'll tell you one more thing that you don't want to hear."

"Let's have it all."

"The Paiutes won't just hit us once and if that don't work give up the fight. To live in this hard desert country, you have to be willin' to keep trying to do a thing over and over. So the Paiutes will just keep comin' at us until either we kill off their whole hunting party, or they kill all of us off."

"Shit," Holt swore. "You've got me worried."

"You should be damned worried," Joe told the man. "And that's why you can't afford not to hire Johnny Redman, and even let me fight beside you if things get really bad and we're startin' to get overrun in a battle."

"Sure! You'd love that!" Holt crowed. "I can see it happening now. I unchain and give you a rifle and when all the Paiutes are shot to hell, then you turn the rifle on me!"

"At least you'd probably die fast," Joe said, not denying that was exactly what he would do given half a chance. "But I'm goin' to kill Eli slow and scalp him while he's still alive."

Holt drove the creaking buckboard for a while without speaking. Finally, he looked at Joe and said, "I am going to hire the half-breed if he shows up this evening. And I'll pay him his due same as I will Eli."

"Sure," Joe said with a chuckle. "And their due will be the same that you're expecting to see me and my wife get paid on the Comstock Lode."

"Aw, just shut the hell up, Joe," Holt growled as they drove on through the dust and the salt flats north of the Great Salt Lake.

✛ 13 ✛

THAT EVENING, JOHNNY Redman slipped into their camp just as quiet as a breeze. The half-breed wasn't there one moment, but he was there the next with his gun in one hand and a rock clenched in the other.

Joe was chained beside Fiona on a wagon wheel facing their campfire. When he saw the half-breed appear, Joe was impressed, for he knew that very few whites other than a few of the old mountain men and Indian scouts could move so stealthily.

"Evenin'," Joe said to the breed. "I'd get up and fix you a plate of beans, pork, and bread, but as you can see I'm chained to this wagon wheel, so I'll just ask Eli to do it for me."

"Gawddamn you, Moss," Eli hissed. "You need to keep your big mouth shut!"

"Stow it!" Holt snapped, looking at the tall young half-breed who was dressed in white man's clothes except for a beaded buckskin belt and his moccasins. "You can holster that gun and drop that rock, Johnny. By the way, why the rock?"

"I can hit a running jackrabbit with a rock," Redman answered. "It saves wastin' bullets, and I can throw this rock hard enough to break a man's skull without a sound."

"And you've killed a man with a rock before?" Holt asked.

"Not yet. But I would have tonight if either you or that other man made a bad move."

"Take it easy," Holt said, managing a smile. "Come have some food. You look as hungry as a winter-starved wolf."

"First we talk," Redman insisted. "Joe told me last night about the bounty you are getting in some faraway place called Virginia City."

"That's right."

"I want a thousand dollars to keep you alive that far," Redman said bluntly. "No less, no more."

"You've probably never had more than twenty dollars altogether at one time in your entire life," Holt told the young Cheyenne.

"It doesn't matter."

"Sure it does," Holt said. "Money ruins Indians."

"I'm half-white, mister."

"I still say that a quick thousand dollars would be your ruination."

"I'll be the one to see about that. I've named my price. You can pay it or I will leave right now."

Holt made a sweeping gesture out toward the huge darkness all around them. "Where would you go out here in this wilderness?"

"I have places to go."

"I'm sure that Perdition would not be one of them," Holt

said. "That was very impressive how you killed the store owner and those two men. I've never seen a man move any faster than you did yesterday."

"I did not want to kill them. They gave me no choice," Redman explained.

"Maybe you did. Maybe you didn't. But what impressed me was that you didn't think on the matter for more than a split second. You're a natural-born killer, son."

"Don't call me son! Don't ever call me son, or savage, or anything but my name, mister! You better call me Johnny or Redman."

"Take it easy!" Holt said, clearly alarmed by this outburst. "All right. I'll call you Johnny, and I've decided that I should pay you to help us get across this desert."

"You made the right decision," the breed said, relaxing. "And just to know that you are a man of your word, I will have that gold pocket watch that you carry."

"What!" Ransom Holt couldn't believe what he'd just heard.

"As a token of our agreement," Redman explained, taking a feather from a leather pouch at his side. "And in return, I will give you this sacred eagle feather."

"Shit!" Holt exclaimed. "That's a damn poor exchange for me. My watch is gold and it cost—"

"I do not care what it cost you, big man. I will return the watch when we get to this place where Man Killer and his woman are to hang. And the value of my eagle feather is great. It cost the lives of two brave Cheyenne warriors."

Holt started to tell the breed that he didn't give a damn if the feather had cost the lives of an entire tribe of Cheyenne. But something in the way Johnny Redman was looking at him and holding the sacred eagle feather gave him second thoughts, and without even understanding why, Holt took the feather while at the same time he handed the young man his expensive timepiece.

"Good," Redman declared with a smile, putting the heavy gold watch up to his ear to listen to it tick. "White men value time more than anything except money. So now that we have exchanged valuable gifts, I know that you and I have an understanding."

"Yes."

"One thousand dollars and I will make sure that you get to this place on the far side of this desert."

"That's it," Holt said, figuring he would kill the breed at the same time that he killed Eli. And then he would take all the bounty as well as get his damned watch back. "Just don't lose my watch before we get there."

In response to those words, Johnny Redman threw back his head and laughed up at the blanket of brilliant stars.

That night, Joe was chained close enough to Fiona to speak to her in private while the others slept. "Fiona, don't get your hopes up too high, but I think that the half-breed will help us."

"You mean help us escape?"

"Maybe," Joe told her. "I'm not sure yet. But I don't think that Johnny Redman has any intention of crossing this entire desert."

"But what about the thousand-dollar reward?" Fiona asked. "That's an awful lot of money."

"Indians don't care that much about money. And Holt was probably right that so much money would bring Johnny to ruin."

"But he's half-white."

"Maybe he is, but there's no doubt in my mind that Johnny Redman is far more of an Indian than a white man."

"So what will we do if he does decide to help us escape?" Fiona asked.

"I don't know yet," Joe admitted. "There's not much that we can do except bide our time and wait for our chance. And anyway, my shoulder is still a long way from being healed, although I'm feelin' stronger every single day."

"Do you think we'll eventually get hanged in Virginia City?" Fiona asked, moving close to her husband. "Tell me the truth."

"I'm sure we won't," Joe said, wanting in the worst way to take his wife in his arms and comfort her fears. "We're just starting this journey across the desert. We ain't even to the headwaters of the Humboldt River yet."

"Where is that?"

"The waters start in the Ruby Mountains. They used to be good trappers' country, but no more."

"How much farther to those Ruby Mountains?"

"Three or four days, I reckon. This next stretch we have to cross is real bad. Damn little water, lots of dust storms, and plenty of murderin' Paiutes. Fiona, you might as well understand right now that it'll be a tough crossing to the Ruby Mountains and a lot of terrible things can happen."

"Do you have friends among the Paiutes?" Fiona asked hopefully. "Paiute friends that would help us get away from Holt and Eli?"

"I have known some Paiutes, and a few of 'em I even trusted. But I can't say that any were my friends. You see, they don't live in big groups or have powerful chiefs like the Plains Indians or some of the other Indians. The Paiutes are really a bunch of small clans that work independent of one another. That's why they're so hard to deal with or for the army to whip. One clan might tell you that you can cross their land if you give 'em something they value . . . but the next clan only fifteen or twenty miles away might have a whole different opinion on the matter and try to put arrows in your horses and your back."

Joe gazed up at the glittering stars. "Fiona, I sure wish that I had my big wolf dog back."

"What wolf dog?" Fiona asked.

"I guess he was only about half wolf," Joe told her. "I picked him up north of Reno when I killed a bounty man while I was hunting for you. Rip became attached to me and stayed by my side when I came back to get you in Virginia City."

"What happened to him?"

"When all hell broke lose by the church and I threw you on that sorrel mare, tellin' you to run for your life, bullets were flying. I killed them two other Peabody brothers and ran into the church, where the priest hid me and Rip in this little cave back behind his altar. The last Peabody brother and what men I hadn't shot and killed searched the church high and low but never found me. But it was dark in that little cave and I didn't realize that Rip had been shot. That big dog died without a whimper by my side and I miss him still."

"He sounds as if he was your very devoted and good friend," Fiona told Joe. "Maybe someday when we are away from all this, you can find another dog like Rip."

"Maybe," Joe said, "but I'm not countin' on it. A dog like that only comes along once or twice in a man's lifetime."

They sat still together gazing up at the stars. "Have you been praying for us, Joe?"

"Me?"

"Yes, you."

Joe shifted on his butt, feeling uncomfortable. "Fiona, you know I'm not a religious man."

"But praying can't hurt."

"No," Joe had to agree, "it can't. It's just that I've never known it to help. So why waste the time prayin' when you should be thinkin' about how to get yourself out of a bad fix like we're in right now?"

"You do the thinking, Joe. I'll do the praying, and maybe between the two of us we can come out of this and get our daughter back."

"It'll happen," Joe vowed. "I'm sure of it. And—"

Joe stiffened.

"What?" Fiona asked with alarm.

"There's men out there in the brush and they're movin' in closer with every intention of killin' us all."

"Joe . . ."

Johnny Redman was awake and on his feet. He kicked Holt and Eli into wakefulness, and then he whispered, "Move back away from the firelight where they can't see you!"

"Indians?" Holt asked.

"Maybe."

Holt was only half awake. "Who the hell else would it be other than Indians?"

"Shhhh! It could be the men from Perdition. Matter of fact, that's probably who is out there."

"What—"

"They want me and they want everything back that you took from them at the store," Johnny explained. "They're professional trackers and killers."

"How many do you think would be out there?"

"At least five or six," Johnny said after a minute. "Maybe as many as a dozen."

"Holt, unchain me and my wife from this wagon wheel so we can hide in the dark!" Joe pleaded. "We're easy targets all lit up by the firelight!"

"I can't do that," Holt said. "Not until we find out how many we're up against."

"Johnny!" Joe hissed. "At least put out that damned fire or my wife and I will be easy first targets!"

Not waiting for Ransom Holt to object, the half-breed

kicked dirt into the fire, smothering it into smoke. Suddenly, the night was very dark except for a little moonlight, and there wasn't a sound.

"Are you sure that someone is out there?" Holt whispered after listening for ten minutes while holding a six-gun in each of his big fists.

"Yes," Johnny Redman said. "But now they know that we know they're here, and they're trying to decide what to do next."

"Maybe we should go after them."

"If you go out there in the sagebrush," the breed said, "you will never come back to this camp alive."

Holt had taken cover behind the buckboard and Eli had done the same.

"So what the hell do we do now?" Eli asked, his whispered voice high-pitched and strained.

"We just hunker down and wait," Joe answered. "If someone has to make the first move, let it be them. And I sure could help you right now if you'd take these shackles off and give me a gun."

"When Hell freezes over!" Holt swore softly. "Now everyone shut up and be ready."

Joe struggled against his shackles and when he realized it was useless, he tried to move closer to shield Fiona from any incoming bullets.

After that, there was nothing to do but wait and see if they were being surrounded by Indians or Jack Mormons. And then to learn what the odds were of them surviving this fight that was most certain to start shortly after dawn.

✦ 14 ✦

JUST AFTER DAWN, a rifle's bullet struck one of their water barrels, and then bullets struck another and another.

"Gawddammit!" Holt shouted into the dawn. "Who are you and what do you want?"

"We're from Perdition and we want what you stole as well as that breed for hangin'!"

"I didn't steal anything!" Holt shouted.

"Yeah, you did! You didn't see that old woman rockin' while she knitted in the back of the store, did you, big man? But she saw *you*. And she heard everything and she says you never paid nothin' for them three big sacks of supplies."

"The old woman is crazy!" Holt bellowed. "I paid for those supplies!"

"Liar! You left our general store while all that commotion was goin' on outside and you stole us blind! That there was a *community* store, big man! That means you stole from each and every one of us in Perdition, and that's a bad, bad offense."

"You're wrong," Holt shouted, his voice no longer sounding blustery or confident.

"Suit your damn self, you thief! But we're not leavin' here until we have you locked up in chains and that breed the same. Then we're takin' you all back to Perdition where you'll be judged!"

"No!" Holt bellowed. "I'm not going anyplace with you outlaw Mormon people."

"Suit yourself, thief!"

Suddenly, it was as if they were caught in the middle of a Civil War battlefield surrounded on all sides by the enemy. Bullets screamed in from every direction so fast that they couldn't even be counted.

"Joe, we're gonna die!" Fiona exclaimed.

Joe Moss swore and surged at his manacles and chains, tearing flesh but otherwise having no effect. "Fiona, scoot behind me as best you can!"

Fiona did that, and Joe had her pretty well covered by his body as the onslaught continued from all around them. He could hear the slugs striking their precious water barrels and water began to run down the bed of the buckboard, spilling on Joe and his wife, then seeping quickly into the bone-dry and dusty earth.

"We can't go far without water!" Joe yelled at Holt, who was hugging the ground near Eli. Both men were trying to spot targets, but failing that, they were shooting blind.

Johnny Redman had scooped out enough dirt so that he was pretty well protected. But the half-breed wasn't firing yet.

"Hold your fire!" Ransom Holt shouted as one of their horses was hit and dropped kicking and squealing in pain. "Gawddammit, stop shooting!"

"Are you gonna surrender yourself and that half-breed?" the same voice as before yelled as the shooting stopped.

Holt sighed deeply, then said, "Yes!"

"You might surrender, but not me!" Johnny Redman hissed, jumping to his feet and diving into the thick brush.

Moments later, Joe heard a startled shout and then a cry of pain. No shots. Just a dull thumping sound and that cry, followed by the sound of a body falling heavily.

"Did the half-breed get away?" Fiona asked.

"Yes," Joe said. "My guess is that the half-breed Cheyenne wasn't lying when he said he could use a rock to knock out a man. Unless I'm mistaken, he's already broken out of the ring surrounding us and is running through the brush like a bobcat staying low and moving fast."

"You better be gettin' to your feet," the voice from the brush shouted. "You won't go anywhere without water and we shot one of your horses, though it was an accident. But it won't be no accident when we shoot you and that half-breed! I'll give you one more minute to stand up and surrender."

"The half-breed is gone!" Holt shouted. "He just jumped up and ran off. It's just me and my hired man and our two prisoners that are here now."

"Stand up and reach for the sky or we'll kill you for certain!"

Holt raged. "Gawddammit!"

"What are we gonna do?" Eli demanded. "We're surrounded."

"The breed got away," Holt shot back. "Eli, maybe you should try and do the same."

"No, sir! I didn't steal from these people and it's not me that they have a bone to pick with. It's *you*, Mr. Holt. And I think you'd best stand up and then see what you can do to make 'em settle down and stop shootin'."

"Shit!" Holt swore, pounding his big fist over and over against the earth.

"What's it to be, thief? You surrendering? Or do you want to end your life and that of your friends right here and now?"

"Surrender!" Eli pleaded. "Dammit, boss, you can talk your way out of this mess!"

Holt unleashed a string of profanities, but knowing he was beaten, he finally shouted, "All right! I'm going to stand up and I don't want anyone to shoot me down."

"Stand up, then, with your hands over your head."

"Get up, Eli!"

"You first, boss."

"You chickenshit sonofabitch!" Holt swore, kicking Eli in the side as he gained his footing.

Eli grunted in pain, but he stayed tight to the ground.

"Now the other one!" the voice called. "Hands up like the big thief."

Eli released the Sharps rifle and stood up slowly, hands up over his head. "I ain't got anything to do with what happened back in Perdition," he screamed into the brush. "So you boys just don't get trigger-happy because I ain't done you no wrong!"

"Joe, what about us?" Fiona asked in a nervous whisper.

"There's nothing we can do," Joe said, his wrists and ankles wet with fresh blood from his struggling to get free of his manacles and chains. "Our fate is in the hands of these rough Jack Mormons."

"Will they hurt or hang us?"

"Depends."

"Depends on *what*, Joe?"

"Depends on what I say and what Holt says and who they finally come to believe." Joe shifted his weight off his wife and leaned back against the wagon wheel.

The Jack Mormons began to stand up all around the camp. One by one, they appeared, armed with rifles and looking grim and prepared to fight to the death to reclaim what had been stolen from their community general store.

"I count fifteen," Joe said. "And I'm sure that there are more on the other side of the wagon that we can't even see yet."

"Holt and Eli wouldn't have stood a chance against so many."

"No," Joe agreed. "If there had been an all-out fight, most likely we'd also have been killed."

The leader of the Jack Mormons was a very tall, very thin man with a long black beard and a blue shirt and a floppy gray hat. He was almost as tall as Ransom Holt, but Joe judged the leader weighed only half as much.

Holt was already talking. "Listen, surely we've got a mis-understanding here, boys. Whatever some old woman said is just plain wrong, or else she's lyin'."

"She's my *ma*," the leader said, eyes narrowing as he raised his rifle to point at Ransom Holt's broad chest. "You callin' my ma a *liar*?"

"No!" Holt cried, realizing what might have been his fatal blunder. "Of course not. I'm just saying that she must not have seen me pay the store owner for the supplies."

"Well, then, she must have stolen the money you paid because it ain't in the cash register or nowhere else in the store." The tall man and his fellow townsmen pressed in closer. "So are you callin' Ma a *thief*?"

"Of course not!"

"Well, then, if she heard you and saw you and there ain't no money to be found . . . well, how kin you explain it, thief?"

"I . . . I . . ."

Ransom Holt didn't have the chance to try to create some explanation for the missing money because the leader slammed upward with the butt of his rifle and it caught Holt on the jaw. The blow was so hard that it knocked Holt a step back into the side of the buckboard.

"Now wait a—"

The man stepped forward fast and struck Holt a second time, and he collapsed in a heap, wet and muddy from the runoff of the riddled water barrels.

"You might have killed him, Ferris."

"I didn't," Ferris said, looking down at Holt. "But him sayin' my ma is a thief and a liar just angered me so bad I had to break his lyin' face."

"He's knocked out cold."

"Tie him up hand and foot, then throw him in the wagon, boys."

"Hey!" a voice called. "Come help us! Caleb is hurt!"

"Go help 'em," the leader ordered three of his men. "And start trackin' that half-breed. When you spot him, shoot him down like you would a rabid dog."

"Don't you want the town to see him hanged for killin' three of our people?"

Ferris considered the question and then shook his head. "The half-breed is gonna be hard to track and harder to kill. So if you get a shot, put him down like a dog, then drag his carcass into Perdition. We'll string up whatever is left of him and that'll satisfy the town."

The three men nodded in agreement, and prepared to get their gear and horses to ride after Johnny Redman. To Joe Moss's way of thinking, if they somehow did track and corner the fleeing half-breed, those three were as good as dead men although they didn't yet realize the fact.

"What about me!" Eli cried, bringing everyone's attention back to himself. "Mister, I didn't steal anything or call your sweet old ma a liar or a thief."

"You climb up into that buckboard and keep your yap

shut. When we get back to Perdition, we'll decide what punishment you should suffer."

"But I didn't . . ." Eli closed his mouth as the leader raised his rifle to bash him in the head. "I'll get in the wagon! Don't have to use that on me, mister. I didn't do any of you Mormons wrong."

It took four men to tie the massive Ransom Holt up and lift him into the buckboard. One of the Jack Mormons put the wounded horse out of its misery, and then they all turned to look down at Joe Moss and Fiona.

"What did you two do to deserve this treatment?" Ferris demanded.

"We didn't do *anything* to deserve it," Joe said through his clenched teeth.

"Don't lie to me, mister!" Ferris hissed, backhanding Joe hard enough to rock his head back on his shoulders. "I already heard all the damned lies I can stand for this month."

"Don't hit him!" Fiona cried, pushing between them. "He's my husband and he hasn't done anything except to try to save my life and get our daughter back from some Catholic nuns in Virginia City."

"You a Catholic?" Ferris asked, his eyes narrowing as he turned them away from Joe to Fiona. "We don't have much likin' for Pope lovers."

"No!" Fiona insisted. "But when I was wrongly accused of murdering a man in Virginia City, I had no choice but to give our little girl to the nuns for safekeeping."

"Of your own free will you gave your little girl over to the damned mackerel eaters?"

"Only for a while. We were trying to get her back when that big man and his friend caught us and put us in chains and manacles."

"What did you do to him and the other one to deserve such ill treatment?"

"Nothing!" Fiona exclaimed. "They're bounty hunters. They were paid to hunt us down and bring us back to Virginia City for hanging."

Ferris leaned close. "You ain't makin' this all up, are you, woman? 'Cause if you are, I'll give you and your husband the same punishments as I'll give the big man who stole from us."

"I swear to you that I'm not making anything up."

Ferris studied Fiona, and then he studied Joe and said, "Boys, get those chains off these two and put 'em in the wagon so all four of 'em are together and easy for us to watch over on the road back to Perdition."

"The keys to our manacles are in the big man's pockets," Joe told the thin and unforgiving Mormon men. "And I thank you for your kindness to me and my wife."

"You'd better hold your thanks, mister. Because we ain't even begun to decide your fates."

"We are innocent," Joe declared, looking at all their faces. "And we have been unfairly chained and mistreated."

"You don't look innocent to me," Ferris told him. "You look like a man who is anything but innocent."

"Punish me if you must," Joe said, "but don't punish my wife."

Ferris must have liked what Joe told him, because he dipped his pointy chin and then walked away. Moments later, Joe and Fiona were unchained and their hated shackles removed.

"You're both gonna have some bad scars," a younger man told them as he inspected their ankle and wrist wounds. "Scars you'll carry the rest of your days."

"We'll live with that," Joe replied, helping his wife to

her feet and then up into the buckboard beside Eli and the still-unconscious Ransom Holt.

"Don't think because we took those chains off that you're out of the woods as to being innocent in our minds," one of the Jack Mormons warned. "We're just holdin' judgment and punishments until we get you back to Perdition and get the truth."

"The truth is that we don't deserve what was done to us by Ransom Holt and Eli," Joe said. "And if it's the truth that you're seekin', then you've just heard it plain."

"Maybe so. There will be a hangin', though. That half-breed has our blood on his hands and he's gonna hang even if they bring him in dead."

Joe didn't have anything to say about that. He would never tell this man that no matter how good the three Jack Mormons sent after Johnny Redman were, they wouldn't be good enough.

"Ma'am," another one of their captors said to Fiona. "You sure are thin and hurt. There are women back in Perdition that can you get to feelin' good and strong again."

Tears welled up in Fiona's eyes, and she nodded with appreciation as the buckboard was being hitched and their lives seemed to have just taken a dramatic turn for the better.

✤ 15 ✤

EIGHT MILES TO the north of the Great Salt Lake and just two hours after Joe and Fiona were placed in the buckboard for a return trip to Perdition and judgment, Johnny Redman found the spot that he had been searching for while on the run.

"It'll do," he said to himself as he entered the deep, fifty-yard-wide arroyo. "It'll do just fine."

The arroyo was an ancient dry riverbed, and it probably had not been flooded in centuries. It was choked with sage and brush and tumbleweeds, and it was as crooked as a sidewinder.

Johnny made sure to leave tracks as he walked into the arroyo and then started hiking north up its course. He had not been able to steal a horse back at the camp when it had come under fire, so he was at a small disadvantage compared to those that were tracking him and were now less than a mile behind. Also, he had not had time to find a rifle, and the Jack Mormons out to get him would surely have rifles that were far better than the two pistols he carried in his holster and waistband.

Out in this desolate, inhospitable country, only a Paiute might survive on foot, and Johnny Redman was no desert Paiute. He didn't know the country and he didn't know the places where scarce, drinkable water could be found. So he needed to get these men off his trail and he needed at least one horse and preferably all of them.

The hunted half-breed would set a trap. If his pursuers left him no choice, maybe a *death* trap.

Johnny moved quickly up the debris-clogged arroyo for about five hundred yards. When it doglegged hard to the right, the half-breed nimbly jumped out of the arroyo and onto a large slab of sandstone, which he then used to carry him up to the rim.

For a moment, he hunkered down and surveyed his path below, noting that he had left tracks, but none so obvious that those who followed him might suspect that they were being purposely led into a trap.

Satisfied, Johnny Redman checked his guns and trotted back along the rim until he came to a big rock near where the arroyo opened to the south. Here he would wait for the men who came to capture or kill him. And once they were inside the arroyo, he would follow them . . . and if they were not too many in number, he would give them the choice—their lives—or their guns and their horses.

The three Jack Mormons were moving at a steady but mile-eating trot and when they came to the arroyo, they paused and one of them dismounted. Johnny was hiding only fifty yards away and he heard one of the men say to the others, "Could be a trap in there."

"Could be," another said, "but we have to be real close to the breed now, and I don't think he's well armed."

"He could be armed," another said, "but he won't have time to think about any trap. He's a runner and he'll keep runnin' until we overtake him. If we dillydally around here, then he's only going to increase his lead on us and we don't want that."

"I agree. Let's go ahead and be real careful. Tom, you watch the rim on the right. Avery, you keep your eyes on the left rim. I'll be lookin' straight ahead. Remember what Ferris said. If we get a shot on the breed, take it and make it count!"

"I'd rather bring him back alive so we can all watch him dance on the end of a rope in Perdition."

"Me, too, but dead is dead and this one needs to be dead."

Johnny overheard this conversation, and now he knew that there were three men who would shoot him on sight and if he was wounded, they would still take him back to be hanged.

The three Mormons rode side by side with their rifles at the ready. Once they were into the arroyo, Johnny Redman slipped out from behind his yellow sandstone rock and crept down behind them.

"Tracks stop here!" one of the men said, dismounting and squatting in the sandy river bottom.

"Are you sure?" Avery asked, also climbing down from his horse along with the third tracker. "The half-breed couldn't have just sprung wings and flown out of this arroyo."

Johnny had moved up fast, and now he was right behind the three. "I didn't. Hands up or I'll shoot all of you in the back!"

The one named Tom spun and tried to bring his rifle to bear on the half-breed, but he took a bullet in the leg for his foolishness. The other two Jack Mormons wisely dropped their weapons into the sandy river bottom and threw up their hands.

"Slow and easy, with your left hands, get your sidearms out of your holsters and toss 'em in my direction."

They did, and then Johnny Redman said, "Tend to your friend because he's bleeding pretty bad."

The two men had obviously been in gunfights before because they didn't waste time or words, but instead put a tourniquet on Tom's leg and then a bandage, which they tied in place with a sweat-soaked bandanna.

Tom was in a lot of pain, but all of them knew he was not going to die . . . unless the young half-breed decided that was what ought to happen next.

"You gonna kill us?" Avery asked.

"You'd have killed me."

"No, we wouldn't have!" Avery lied. "We were just going to—"

"Shut up!" Johnny ordered, cocking back the hammer of his gun and noting how their frightened horses were trotting back toward the mouth of the arroyo. "Now back away from Tom and turn around to face the wall."

"He's gonna shoot us in the back!" Avery cried, turning pale.

"No, I'm not," Johnny told the man. "But I have cause to do that, which you would have done to me."

"Then what are you going to do with us?"

Johnny twisted around and saw that the horses had slowed to a walk and were now nibbling at what little grass there was to be found. They weren't that far away, and he knew that he could easily catch them. "I'm going to let you find your own way out of this hellish country," he decided aloud. "While I ride off with your guns and your horses."

"What!" Avery turned despite the orders and cried, "Good gawd, man! We're miles and miles from Perdition.

Without horses or guns, we're as good as dead men. Paiutes will find and kill us if we don't die of thirst!"

Johnny Redman wanted to tell Avery that, with a lot of luck and pluck, they just might make it out of this desert to safety, but to do so they might have to leave the wounded tracker named Tom.

Instead, he told the three Jack Mormons, "All right. You were going to shoot me down without a second thought, but I'm going to give you a fighting chance to live. I'll leave a horse, your rifles, and canteens about a mile south of here."

"Just one horse?" Avery asked. "But—"

"One horse for your stupid friend Tom. And canteens and all your rifles for the Paiute, if they find you before you get back to your settlement and families."

Avery blew out a deep breath of relief. "If you're really gonna do that, then maybe you ain't as terrible as you acted when you gunned those three down in Perdition."

"They had it coming," Johnny said. "But you'd never believe that since they were your own kind and I'm a half-breed."

"Half-breed or not, you're treatin' us white," Avery replied. "I just wish you'd leave us with all three of our horses."

"Well, I won't leave you but one for Tom to ride and you two fellas to lead," Johnny told them. "And if you make it to Perdition, tell the others that those killings I did were all in self-defense. It was me or them and no man is gonna allow himself to be killed without trying to kill first."

Avery nodded. "That big man that you were with, he stole three sacks of supplies from us."

"That's none of my concern."

"He's probably gonna hang or at least taste the lash."

"He deserves both, and so does the one called Eli."

"What about the mountain man and his woman?"

"They're innocent of everything except they killed some rich brothers who won't stop until they are hanged on the Comstock Lode."

"Were you gonna help deliver them to the noose?"

"I was," Johnny admitted. "There was a handsome reward for my gettin' them across this hellish desert."

"What are you gonna do now?" Avery finally asked.

Johnny Redman chuckled. "I'm not gonna be so dumb as to tell you my plans . . . that's for damn sure!"

"You gonna—"

"Enough talk," Johnny said, anxious to be on his way. "Don't try to follow me ever again or the next time I'll kill you faster than you can blink."

"We won't," Avery promised. "None of us will follow you again."

"That's what I wanted to hear you say," Johnny told them. "And if you make it back to Perdition, I want you to tell the big man I haven't quit the job."

"Meanin'?"

"Meaning that I'll be seeing him later, if you don't decide to string him up by the neck with a stout rope."

"So you're gonna try and collect that reward money?"

"Yep. I got a big need for a thousand dollars."

"A thousand!"

"That's right."

"That rich man in Virginia City must have a powerful lot of hatred in his heart."

"I would say so," Johnny agreed. "Now why don't we quit talking and you boys start back for home. It'll be a long walk."

"We can do 'er," Avery vowed as he walked over to his friend and said, "Let's get Tom on his feet and start back to Perdition. We'll go slow and easy on the horse this half-breed has promised to leave us. That's what you promised, right?"

But Johnny Redman didn't hear the question. He was already trotting out of the arroyo with a mind to catch up with the Mormon horses. One he would leave behind, along with guns and water. But the other pair—the best two of the three—were now his own to ride in whichever direction he wanted out of this miserable desert.

Trouble was, Redman wasn't exactly sure where he wanted to go anymore, but damned if that thousand-dollar bounty wasn't mighty tempting.

✛ 16 ✛

Two days later, Joe Moss and Fiona were standing before an old, gray-bearded elder of Perdition named Ira Young who solemnly informed them that he was a distant cousin of their Salt Lake City prophet, Brigham Young. Joe and Fiona had no horses, weapons, or money, so they were pretty much stuck waiting to see what these people would do either to or for them. They had been given a private room, baths, fresh clothes, all the food they could eat, and little else. But now, bathed and free of their chains and shackles, Joe and Fiona felt as if they had died and gone to heaven.

"What we are going to do today," Ira Young pronounced to most of the population of his small Mormon settlement, "is determine the proper punishment for Mr. Ransom Holt and his friend, Eli Brown."

Eli, like Ransom Holt, was standing before the old patriarch with his hands bound behind his back and his feet stripped of shoes.

Eli cried, "But sir, I ain't done no wrong to you folks!

When I was here, I didn't do anything but watch over our prisoners!"

Ira Young wore spectacles on his long, hooked nose, and now he gazed down at them and snapped, "You will be silent or you will be horsewhipped! Is that understood, Mr. Brown?"

"Yes, sir," Eli said, swallowing hard and then bowing his head.

Ira Young was seated on a big wooden chair that was placed on an upraised platform in a large schoolroom. Joe reckoned the schoolhouse was large because Mormons tended to have a lot of young'uns. The spacious schoolroom with a big potbellied stove in the center of its floor apparently doubled as Perdition's meeting hall. Now the room was packed and it was stifling hot.

"What do you think Mr. Young will do to Holt and Eli?" Fiona whispered to Joe.

"I don't know and I don't care," Joe replied. "Just as long as they let us go in peace and give us some travelin' money."

"Do you expect them to do that?"

"I don't," Joe confessed. "But we can always ask."

Ira Young cleared his throat and seemed keenly aware that he had the complete attention of everyone in the big schoolroom. "Now then," he said, gazing at Ransom Holt with something akin to disgust, "what we folks in this town know for sure is that you *stole* three sacks of valuable supplies from our community store."

"I didn't do that!" Holt shouted. "I paid for those supplies!"

"If that be so, where did your money go?" Smith demanded, his voice causing heads in the room to nod. "Because you see, Grandma Parsons sure hasn't got it, and even if she did, she'd have no place to spend it except in our own

general store. So I ask you, Mr. Holt, where is the money you
spent for all those valuable supplies?"

"I . . . I don't know." Holt took a ragged breath. He was
in deep trouble and knew it. "Maybe someone else was in
the store and took that money."

Ira Young didn't appreciate that answer even a little bit.
"There are no other thieves in Perdition other than yourself."

"Well . . . well, maybe my man Eli got into the store without my knowing it and took the money."

"What?" Eli cried in shock and outrage. "Mr. Holt, you
know that never happened. You told all of us after we left
that you stole those supplies. You even *bragged* about stealing those supplies."

Holt was tied, but he was far from cowed or being harm-
less. He swung around, lowered his great bull head, and
drove it squarely into Eli's face, breaking his nose and knocking the smaller man into the crowd.

Eli howled in pain. In response to Holt's behavior, the
furious Jack Mormons clubbed the giant to his knees, and
might have beaten him to death if Ira Young had not ordered them to stand back.

"Mr. Moss!"

Joe was instantly alert to the judge. "Yeah?"

"Did you or your wife overhear Mr. Holt bragging about
how he stole those three sacks of valuable supplies from
us?"

"I did," Joe said in complete honesty.

"Did you hear the same, Mrs. Moss?"

"Yes," Fiona answered, her voice loud enough to be
heard by the entire roomful of avid listeners. "It was when
we were in the buckboard about two miles out of this town.
Ransom bragged, making it clear that he was quite proud of
the fact that he'd gotten all the supplies we needed without

payment. And that he'd done it while three men were being shot down by the half-breed so that everyone was distracted."

The audience erupted in anger and some of the men surged at Holt, who was dazed from the beating he'd just suffered.

"Stay back!" Ira Young bellowed, jumping up from his chair with surprising agility. "I say stay back and I will make a pronouncement on the fate of this pair."

The crowd backed off a little, and Ira Young pushed his spectacles up and said, "You, Mr. Holt, should hang for your thievery, but I will show mercy and you will be given thirty lashes with a bullwhip on your stripped back and buttocks."

"No!" Holt bellowed, trying to lunge at the old man. "No man will whip me!"

"You will suffer a just punishment for your thievery. Whether you agree with me or not, I have shown you great mercy, Mr. Holt. I could have decreed your death sentence."

"And what about me!" Eli cried as the blood seeped from his nose.

"Fifteen lashes with the bullwhip!"

"No!' Eli sobbed, almost falling to his knees. "I didn't steal from you. I have done no wrong and deserve no punishment."

Ira raised a finger and pointed it at the smaller man. "When your camp west of Perdition was overrun at dawn, you fired on Ferris and our men. You shot to kill my brethren and so you shall pay."

"But that was because they were firing at us!"

Ira Young waved the protest off like he would a pesky fly. "Fifteen whiplashes, Mr. Eli Brown. No more. No less."

"Oh, sweet Jesus!" Eli whimpered, tears streaming down his face. "Oh, my Lord, I can't bear that!"

"You will live and you will have learned your lesson well when you leave Perdition."

Joe Moss and Fiona were brought forward. Joe had to admit that his heart was pounding like a Cheyenne warrior's drum when he planted his feet on the schoolhouse floor and took Fiona's hand in his own.

"Now," Ira Young said, his voice softening. "There is the far more complicated matter of you and Mrs. Moss. What do you have to say for yourselves?"

Joe was not a man of many words, so he left out the preliminaries and went right to the heart of the issue. "I killed two brothers named Peabody in Virginia City when they tried to kill me. My wife is accused of killin' another Peabody, but she didn't."

The elder turned his eyes on Fiona. "What say you, Mrs. Moss? Did you kill a man named Peabody?"

"I definitely did not!" Fiona said, raising her chin. "It is, however, true that Mr. Chester Peabody was found dead in my little shack on the Comstock Lode. But only because I brought him in from outside in the dark of night and tried to save his life."

"It would seem," Ira Young said, eyes narrowing with suspicion, "that a Virginia City jury thought otherwise."

"It was a jury bought and paid for by a vengeance-minded family of rich mine owners. I was poorly counseled and represented in the court, and the sentence I received from a judge secretly paid off by the Peabody family was entirely unfair and unjust."

"So you say, Mrs. Moss. So you say."

Ira Young momentarily turned his attention back to Ransom Holt and Eli Brown. In a voice that sounded like doom, he roared, "Take these two out of my presence and administer their just and well-deserved punishments!"

Holt kicked the first Mormon right between the legs,

and the man went down howling. Despite having his hands tied behind his back, Ransom Holt tried to charge and kill Ira Young possibly with his teeth. Men piled on Holt's broad back and drove him down to the floor, and then they struck him with their fists until he was unable to move.

Eli stood nearby as white as a bedsheet, and cried until he was shoved out of the schoolhouse. When Ransom Holt was also half carried out to receive his punishment, Ira Young relaxed.

"Now then," the old man said, drumming his fingers. "As I said earlier, your situation is far more complicated and unclear to me. On the one hand, you were being taken to hang in Virginia City, but on the other hand, you claim that the only blood you shed was in self-defense."

"I swear that is true," Fiona said.

"Hmm, perhaps," Young mused, "you actually did perform an act of mercy that was judged wrongly."

"That is exactly what happened," Fiona said, while Joe nodded in agreement.

Ira Young said, "But we have no witnesses and no proof of either your guilt or your innocence. And since neither of you were physically able to steal from us or fire upon my people, as did Mr. Holt and Mr. Brown, I have no choice . . . no choice but to absolve you of any wrongdoing or injury."

Joe's knees almost buckled with relief. He crushed his wife's hand and said, "Sir, I shore do appreciate your good thinkin' and justice. Now, if I kin say one more thing, when we was taken by Holt and Eli, I had money, weapons, and horses. I'd like them returned to me from what they had when you took 'em prisoner."

"I have no proof of what you are telling me, Mr. Moss."

"But . . . but you know that no man is gonna have no guns, nor money, nor horses. So—"

"There are plenty of men and even families who come through Perdition on their way to California or the Comstock Lode and they are penniless and weaponless."

"But—"

"Mr. Moss, understand something. Since you cannot possibly prove that anything was taken from you either by Mr. Holt or Mr. Brown, then I cannot possibly give anything back to you. Unless—"

"Unless what?" Fiona asked.

"Unless either of those men want to swear to me that they took your weapons, money, and horses."

"They would rather die first," Joe said. "They'd never tell you anything that wasn't to their own selfish benefit."

"Well," Ira Young said, throwing up his hands in a gesture of indifference, "then all I can give you is what has already been given. Your clothing and the food you have eaten. And unless you wish to remain here and work for your keep, then I order you both banished from Perdition."

Joe swallowed. "Sir," he said, "you know that we can't just walk out into that desert without anything but our clothes."

Ira Young was losing his patience. "Then both of you walk back to wherever you came from and be gone from this place!"

Joe could see that the elder of Perdition was getting upset with him and that things could be far worse, so he managed to nod his head and said, "Can we just go now?"

"You can and never, ever come back."

"That ain't a bit likely," Joe told the Mormon leader. "And . . . I'd be obliged if you'd hold those two for a spell after their whiplashings. Thataway, me and the missus would have some time to put some distance between them and us."

Ira Young actually smiled for the first time. "I can assure

you both that, after my sentence, neither of those men will be in any condition to chase after you for a good many days."

Joe tried one more time. "Judge, I sure would like just one gun, and there's a 'hawk that they took from me, and—"

"A tomahawk?"

"Yes, sir."

"It was shown to me, Mr. Moss. And that is *your* weapon?"

Joe nodded vigorously. "It sure is! I've had it for some time and I've taken many a scalp with—"

Fiona banged her husband hard in the ribs. "Shhh!"

Ira Young's mouth was hanging open in disbelief.

"Never mind what my husband said. It is his tomahawk and he does prize it, but he'd never use it to take a scalp or a life."

"I see," Young said, clearly not seeing what was true or untrue. "Well, then, you shall have your tomahawk returned as well as one pistol with six rounds in the chamber."

"A good pistol?"

"A loaded pistol," Smith said. "And used but good shoes for walking as far and as fast as you can from this place."

Joe folded his arms across his broad chest. "And a couple of canteens of water would sure be helpful, Judge."

"You're pushing me too hard, Mr. Moss. But I will grant your request and you shall ask for no more than to be gone from Perdition within the fifteen minutes . . . or even less."

"We'll do 'er," Joe promised with a wide grin. "Although I'd sorta have liked to see them two get the bullwhip put to their murderin' hides."

"Be gone!" Ira Young exclaimed.

Fiona nearly yanked Joe off his feet and dragged him outside the schoolhouse. A few minutes later, they were given a loaded gun, two pair of hard-used shoes that didn't fit well,

and two large canteens filled with good water. Lastly, someone handed Joe his treasured tomahawk, asking, "Can you
throw that thing with any accuracy?"

"I wish I could throw it at Holt," Joe said, watching as
the giant was being tied to a tree and stripped of his shirt,
then having his breeches dropped to his knees in prepara-
tion for his brutal whipping. "I could split his big skull like
a melon and then I'd scalp the bastard."

Joe's voice was so angry that the Jack Mormon backed
away and said, "Just leave this place while you are allowed."

"We'll do 'er," Joe said, stuffing the tomahawk behind
his belt and beside an old but serviceable cap-and-ball pistol that had been used hard and often.

Suddenly, the punishments for Ransom Holt and Eli
Brown began with the sharp whistle of a bullwhip. The pair
were tied to a post and with each lash of the bullwhip, Eli
screamed to the mountaintops while Holt simply cursed.

Joe Moss paused for a minute to watch the whippings,
and there was already blood all over the stripped backs and
buttocks of both men.

"Oh, God," Fiona said with a trembling voice. "I can't
bear to watch."

"If I could, I would take the whip and use it on them until they were nothing but red meat and bone," Joe declared.
"And then I'd scalp 'em both while they was just barely
alive."

"Joe, let's go now!" Fiona pleaded as Eli screamed again
when the lash bit deeply into his flesh. "Please!"

Joe nodded and had his last, satisfying look at what he
considered to be justice fairly served. He knew that this pair
would survive the lashings, although Eli could not have
taken Holt's thirty and be left with a sane mind.

As Joe and Fiona passed by the whipping post and the
two men, Holt's head whipped around and through bloody

teeth he screamed, "I'll find you, Joe Moss! And I'll find your woman! I found you both once and I won't ever stop until I find you again and see you—"

Whatever else Ransom Holt had to say died in a moan as the lash ripped flesh from his exposed buttocks. The huge man bent like a branch in the wind, and then he straightened up, threw back his shaggy head, and cursed the sun and the sky until the next lash struck his massive, trembling body.

✛ 17 ✛

J OE AND FIONA left Perdition even before the brutal
lashings of Ransom Holt and Eli Brown were finished.
They could hear Eli scream every time the bullwhip
struck his back or buttocks, and the awful sound didn't stop
until they were both well out of Perdition.

"Where are we going, Joe?" Fiona asked. "Nevada is to
the west, but you're leading us east."

"There are people watching," Joe said, jacking a thumb
back toward the town they'd just left. "You can be sure that
word will get back to Ransom Holt that we headed back
into the Wasatch Mountains."

"But why east?"

"Fer two reasons," Joe said as they walked swiftly toward
the high, blue mountains. "One bein' that even with a few
days head start, we wouldn't get far in that desert with only
two full canteens and an old pistol. We'd either die of thirst
or the Paiutes would kill us for certain. An' you can't hide
your tracks out there in that desert."

"And the other reason?"

"I trapped in the Wasatch for two years," Joe told her. "And even more important, I know some of the Indians up in those mountains. I expect they'll help us even if those folks in Perdition didn't."

"We got a very fair shake from Ira Young," Fiona said. "I was deathly afraid that they might hang or lash us like they did Ransom Holt and Eli Brown."

"We got off free because we were shackled and chained all the time we were in Perdition so there was no way that Ira Young could say we might have been in on the thievery."

Fiona looked at her wrists, which were chafed bloody from the manacles she'd worn. "I'm going to carry these scars for the rest of my life. So are you, Joe."

"Scars are just the badges you earn for livin'," Joe told her. "Show me a man or a woman without scars and I'll show you someone who ain't done squat. Anyway, you're still gonna be a pretty woman."

"But I'm not now because I'm so skinny and—"

Joe stopped and hugged his poor wife. "Fiona, you've gone through hell and I hate to say it, but we've still got a hard row to hoe before we can ever expect to get our daughter back. Ransom and Eli will be comin' after us once they heal from the bullwhippin'. You heard what Holt yelled at us back there. He ain't one to give up."

"Maybe Eli will, though."

"I expect Holt will talk or force Eli to stick with him in chasin' us down," Joe said. "I don't reckon Holt wants to go against me one on one."

"What can we do when they come?"

"Well," Joe said, releasing his wife. "The first time they caught you, I wasn't with ya. Then they caught me because I was alone. So the way I'm figurin' it, if we stick together and use our noggins, maybe we can get through all this. But I'll expect t' kill 'em both."

"That won't be easy, Joe."

"No," he admitted. "It won't be, but there is no choice. They won't stop huntin' us and we can't run forever. They know that sooner or later we're gonna show up at St. Mary's Church in Virginia City to collect our daughter."

"What about the half-breed?" Fiona asked. "What about Johnny Redman?"

Joe almost smiled. "He's the joker in the deck. He's the only one that I haven't been able to figure. He's a half-breed, and generally those kinds of men just want to stay away from whites and even from their own people. They don't fit in with either the white man's or the Indian's world, and they don't care a good damn about money."

"But Johnny was interested in the bounty on our heads."

"So he told Ransom Holt," Joe commented. "But I'm not sure that the bounty of a thousand dollars is why Johnny Redman signed on with Holt."

"What other reason then?"

"Maybe none. Maybe something. I don't know. I just figure we haven't seen the last of that half-breed."

"Do you think he'll try to capture us and take us to the Comstock so that he can collect the entire reward?"

"He just might be thinking that way," Joe said, consciously making an effort not to walk so fast that Fiona couldn't keep up without trotting next to him.

"I hope not. I hope we never see or hear from Redman again."

"I'll second that," Joe agreed. "That half-breed is a dangerous, dangerous man."

That evening, tired and exhausted from all their walking, Joe and Fiona made a cold camp in the foothills of the Wasatch Range. Fiona was limping badly because her ill-fitting Mormon shoes had given her flaming red blisters.

Joe was limping for the same reason, and he knew that they had to get better shoes or boots and some food and supplies.

At dusk, he shot a big mountain jackrabbit with the Colt Navy, and used two sticks to rub together to finally get a cooking fire under way. Joe gutted the rabbit and they roasted it on sticks. They had used both canteens of their Perdition water while getting off the salt flats, but there was a clear stream coming off the mountains and the water tasted delicious.

"Joe," Fiona said. "I can't wear these awful old shoes any longer, and I can't walk over this rocky ground in my bare feet. I've gone lame."

"I'll make you a moccasin out of this rabbit skin. Gonna need to shoot another for the second foot, though."

"You were married to an Indian woman once," Fiona said. "Did she make moccasins out of rabbit pelts?"

"Nope. A rabbit's hide ain't tough enough to stand up to much hard travel."

"Then maybe we ought to find a little settlement and see if we can work a few days to get enough money for shoes and supplies."

"Maybe," Joe said, not sounding too keen on the idea. "But I hate to lose any of our head start on Holt and Eli."

"I know what you mean. But what choice do we have?"

"If we come upon a settlement, then I might be able to win some money in a card game."

Fiona raised an eyebrow in question. "You don't have any money to bet."

"I could bet this old Colt Navy."

"It isn't worth much."

"No," Joe agreed, "but it'll buy me a few hands and if I'm lucky, I could build up the winnin's."

"But if you're unlucky at the cards, then we don't even have a weapon with which to defend ourselves."

"Not true," Joe said with a grin. "I got my 'hawk and I can defend the hell out of us with it."

Fiona squeezed his arm. "I just won't abide you taking any more scalps, Joe. Killing someone in self-defense is one thing, but scalping is quite another. Please tell me that scalping is now in your past."

"Oh, hell," Joe said. "If it really troubles you, then I won't scalp no more men. But many was the time I'd pull a good scalp from my pouch and trade it for useful things."

"Joe?"

"All right," he said. "No more scalpin'. But the 'hawk will protect us in troubles, Fiona. Trust me on that."

"I do."

"That's good to know."

The following morning, Joe used another one of his six precious bullets to shoot another jackrabbit, which they again roasted and devoured. Then he skinned the animal and used a strand of the rabbit's gut to sew a pair of crude moccasins for Fiona.

"But, Joe, they're still slick with blood and fat!" she protested, making a face as he laced them on her poor, blistered feet.

"Better the pelts are that way than your feet," Joe said. "And you won't have to wear 'em for long. We're avoidin' Salt Lake City and the farms around here, but as we move into these mountains we'll find folks and work things out."

"I sure hope so."

"Ya got t' trust me and yourself," Joe told her. " 'Cause that's all we got left to believe in."

"No," Fiona countered, "we've got our *daughter*."

"Tha's right," Joe said with a smile. "And don't you ever let me forget that."

"Believe me, I won't."

Late on the afternoon of the second day, now deep into the high mountains, they faintly heard a rifle shot, and shortly afterward saw vultures circling in the sky. Joe said, "Probably a hunter shot some deer meat."

"Should we just avoid him?"

"Nope. Sharing your meat is the rule of the mountains. Some don't want to do it, but I always did and this fella will, too . . . one way or 'nother."

It took them an hour of moving through heavy timber and over and around big rocks before they climbed up to a point where they looked down and saw a dead man being eaten by a sow grizzly bear and her cub. "Oh," Fiona cried, covering her eyes. "How awful!"

"Awful for him," Joe said, "but good for us."

"Are we just going to stand here and let that man be eaten?"

"I reckon so," Joe replied. "The sow and her cub will eat for a while, then scratch and kick dirt over the body. They'll go away to sleep and come back later to eat more."

"I think I'm going to be sick," Fiona told her husband as she covered her mouth and turned away to retch.

Instantly, the sow heard the unfamiliar sound, and its massive head whipped around just as Joe pushed Fiona to the earth and they huddled out of the grizzly's sight.

After a few minutes, the sow returned to her gorging. Her cub had never stopped.

For the next two hours the bears stayed next to the dead man, eating off his legs, arms, and a buttock. The sow, with her long claws, ripped off the man's clothes, and when the two grizzly bears were filled with fresh meat, they finally ambled off into the trees.

"You wait right here," Joe told Fiona. "That man had a rifle and probably a six-gun. Too bad for him that he wasn't a better shot."

"You're going down there to strip him?" Fiona's face displayed shock and revulsion.

"You betcha," Joe told her. "And if we're real lucky, he's got a camp and a horse tied up not too far away."

"Bury him, Joe. Please bury the poor soul."

"I can't take the time," Joe told her. "That momma bear isn't going to go far from her kill. I'll have to slip in fast and get out even faster."

"If the man had a rifle, you could . . ."

"It's empty," Joe told her. "That's the shot we heard a while ago. I reckon the fella will have a pistol, but I already got one and ain't no pistol gonna stop a ragin' momma griz."

"Be careful!"

"I will," Joe vowed. "I do have my 'hawk, you know."

"That's no match for a grizzly bear."

"Well, I reckon that's true enough," Joe told her as he headed down the slope toward the half-eaten body.

It took him nearly a half hour to reach the dead man, and it wasn't a pretty sight. The vultures had already landed on the body and begun picking out the eyes and protruding tongue. Joe scared them off, but they didn't fly far, and some only hopped away a short distance and screeched at him in anger.

The man had been middle-aged and his eyesight must have been poor because he was still wearing a pair of spectacles, although they were now covered with blood and one of his round lenses was missing.

Joe wasted no time at the sow's fresh kill. With the gore-splattered vultures screeching and hissing at him, Joe went through the man's blood-soaked pockets and found seventeen dollars and change. He also stripped off the man's gun belt and pistol, this one the heavier Colt Army .45. Joe removed chewing tobacco, a pocketknife, and a nice hunting knife from the remains. He searched for a wallet or some identification, but he didn't expect to find any and did not.

Lastly, Joe pulled off the dead man's boots, which looked as if they might be a good fit, along with his socks. Joe would have liked to take the man's coat, but it was too ripped up and bloody, so he left it. But the real prize was the Spencer rifle and its bullets, which were spilled close by the body. With a rifle and ammunition, Joe knew that he could now shoot all the meat that he and his wife needed to survive in the mountains.

"I thank you for your belongings, mister. Sorry I can't tell your kinfolk what became of you," he whispered to the corpse. "But then again, they'd probably not want to know about your bad ending."

Suddenly, the sow grizzly burst out of the trees with her cub following right behind. When she saw Joe, she reared up on her hind legs and snarled, showing long fangs and slinging saliva back and forth.

"I was just leavin'," Joe told her, backing away fast from her kill. "Just right now I'm leavin'."

Joe continued to back up and reload the Spencer. Once he had a bullet in the breech, and with two cap-and-ball pistols already loaded, he was more than confident that he could shoot the sow and her cub and feast well on bear meat that night.

But for some reason, he didn't want to kill the mother bear or her cub. "It's your prize," he said to the pair. "And you've done us a big favor, so I'm gonna just leave you and your cub in peace . . . if you'll allow it t' be that away."

The sow stopped advancing and snapping her glistening

teeth. She watched Joe retreat back down the mountainside into the trees and brush before returning to her kill.

"Look what I got us!" Joe said, barely able to conceal his joy. "Fiona, we got a whole new lease on life now!"

"What about that poor, poor man?"

"He's gone from this world," Joe said. "He ain't in no pain and he's passed on to us many good things."

"I still wish we could at least bury his remains."

"The sow will bury what she don't eat, and then the vultures and the varmints will eat and scatter what little is left. What we got to do is to find the man's camp."

"How do you know he has one?"

"He didn't have a pack nor bedroll. He was pretty well dressed and I got seventeen dollars cash off'n his body, so he would have a horse and outfit. The horse will be tied someplace in the trees, and we got to find it before the sow or another grizzly does. Once we do that, you won't have to worry about your poor feet no more because you'll be ridin' high!"

Fiona managed a sad smile. "I just wish it wasn't at that poor man's expense."

"He should never have been out here on foot in heavy timber knowin' he couldn't see well nor shoot any better," Joe said without condemnation. "His mistake cost him his life, but it might have saved ours."

"Let's find the horse and try not to find any grizzly bears," Fiona said.

"Fiona, kin you walk a mile or two in those new rabbit moccasins I made you?"

"I sure can." Fiona shielded her eyes and looked up at the circling vultures, then shivered. "Let's go!"

It didn't take Joe Moss more than an hour of brush beating to locate the dead man's camp. His horse was a strawberry roan, and a nice one at that. The bedroll was newly bought and well made. There were pots and pans and a little burro that was bawling and scared half out of its wits. Tied up to an aspen like the roan, the burro was so upset that it had wound itself around and around the tree until its shaggy little head was tethered tight against the white bark.

"What's he so upset about?" Fiona asked as Joe got the pack animal straightened out and then laid a soothing hand on its trembling hide.

"The burro is maybe a little smarter than the strawberry," Joe explained. "And it knows there's a grizzly out there, and maybe it even smells the dead man's blood."

"What are we going to do now?"

"Let's pack the burro, saddle the horse, and cover as much ground as we can before dark," Joe decided. "That griz has tasted human flesh, and once they do that they'll come for you near every time they get hungry."

"Then let's hurry!"

"I'm a-fixin' to do 'er," Joe told his wife as he sat down and pulled the new socks and then boots on. "Damned if that dead fella didn't have big feet like me!"

"Joe, please let's hurry."

Joe jumped up and started packing the skittish burro. Once he had that done to his satisfaction, he saddled the strawberry roan, then glanced at Fiona's legs and adjusted the stirrups to her length.

"Mount up," he said, holding the roan's reins.

The strawberry was a tall, handsome animal and Fiona was not a tall woman, so she really had to stretch to climb up into the saddle. But once that was done, she asked for the reins and the strawberry proved to be as gentle as a child's pony.

"He'll do you fine," Joe judged, picking up the lead on their new pack burro and starting off. "We'll go a ways to the south and when we're well clear of the Salt Lake, we'll cut back to the west and into the big basin desert."

Joe looked back, and seeing his poor, abused wife astride the nice strawberry roan made his heart feel good and proud. A man should always take care of the woman he loved, and Joe felt as if he had done a few things right in the last couple of days to take care of Fiona. She still looked pretty awful from all the starvation and ill treatment she'd received, but Joe knew that she was stronger than she appeared and would begin to fill out and mend.

"What about water?" Fiona called out.

"Water?"

"Yes, Joe. Water. If we're going back into the desert, we'll have to have lots of good water."

"That's for sure."

"Well?" Fiona asked. "We sure don't want to go out into the desert and die of thirst. That's probably a terrible way to die."

"It is," Joe said. "It's about the worst I ever saw."

"You saw someone die of thirst?"

"A partner long ago. I nearly joined him . . . but that's not worth the tellin' and it's a bad story."

"Then how will we survive until we reach the Humboldt River?"

"I'll find water holes along the way there," he promised. "Either that, or I'll pay some Paiute to lead us to the hidden desert water holes. And after a while, we'll get to the Ruby Mountains, and then we'll traipse on down to the Humboldt River and follow it all the way to the Comstock Lode."

"But what if that's exactly what Ransom Holt and Eli expect and they're waiting to catch us?"

"Then they're just waiting to die, darlin'," Joe said, leading the little burro out of camp and striking south. He raised his new Spencer and yelled back to Fiona, "Yes, Missus Moss, if that's their plan, then they're just waitin' to die."

"But no scalps, Joe," Fiona reminded him.

"No scalps," he agreed with a hearty laugh and a new spring to his step.

✛ 18 ✛

R ANSOM HOLT FELT the shackles at his wrists being removed, and he stared up at the clear blue sky, wondering if he should strike out and kill as many of these men of Perdition as possible, or use his wits and survive.

He chose to use his wits.

"There you go," Ferris said, stepping back quickly with a gun in his fist. "Our womenfolk have tended to and salved your back and buttocks, but I reckon you'll carry the scars of being a thief forever."

Ransom barely trusted himself to speak as he came to his feet and swayed unsteadily. "Where is Eli Brown?"

"He's being dressed and is comin'. Ira Young wants you both out of Perdition before the sun sets."

"We'll be gone."

"Just don't ever come back," Ferris warned. "If you do, you'll be shot on sight."

Ransom ground his teeth, thinking that returning someday to kill this man would be at the top of his list.

"You hear me, thief?"

"I hear you," Ransom hissed. "But I want my horses, mules, weapons, and buckboard back. They are mine and gawddammit, I will have them! Or are you people hypocrites as well as being thieves?"

"You can have 'em back," Ferris said. "You'll get everything that's yours. But we took a horse for the supplies you used and the water barrels."

"You're the ones that shot holes in them!"

"Yep. But we're taking them into account," Ferris said. "Them shot-up water barrels are still in your buckboard, and there's bound to be some water left in their bottoms that didn't leak out. But were I you, I wouldn't be arguin' so much, but instead gettin' out of this town."

"Give me my weapons!" Holt demanded.

Ferris looked over at his friends, who were also armed and prepared to fight. Then he turned back to Holt and said, "We don't trust puttin' loaded weapons in your hands, mister. So you and your partner will find 'em along with the rest of your lawful belongings out in the desert about a mile west of Perdition."

"So we're supposed to walk out there in our condition?"

"That's right. Walk or crawl. It don't matter to us, thief."

Ransom had to turn away for a moment; otherwise, he would have attacked this self-righteous Jack Mormon bastard. It had been five days since his flesh had been ripped from his backside by a bullwhip, and Ransom had never known so much pain. In all that time, the only thought on his mind was to somehow get revenge against these people who had humiliated him and lashed him bloody. And he would do that, but later, when he was physically able to do so with some good hired gunmen.

"Here," Ferris said, handing Ransom Holt a can of grease or lard. "My sister said to give it to you and your man. You put it on each other's backs and buttocks and it'll help heal the wounds and keep the flies away."

Holt didn't bother to say thanks. He moved unsteadily to the door and then wobbled out into the street, looking around at this town that he would one day find a way to destroy.

"Just remember that Ira Young could have had you hanged," Ferris said from behind him. "He had the right, being as you're nothin' but a thief."

"Fuck you!" Holt hollered. "Fuck you and this whole rotten fucking town!"

The hatred and vehemence in his voice surprised even himself, and the Mormon backed up, raising his gun and pointing it at Holt. "You shouldn't say those bad and dirty words against us, thief! You got what you deserved. Maybe this taught you a lesson and you won't steal ever again."

"Get Eli Brown out here and don't you dare lecture me!"

Ferris blushed with anger, and then he turned and disappeared while Holt tried to calm down. He was weak and dizzy from both pain and the loss of blood, and he knew that Eli, who had taken just half as many lashes, would be in equally bad shape. Moments later, when Eli did appear, Holt was shocked by the man's pale and haggard appearance.

"Eli," Holt said, "are you gonna make it?"

"I . . . I am," Eli finally whispered. "But let's shake the dust of this hellhole and get before they do decide to hang us both."

"They've taken our horses and buckboard and everything else we own out into the desert a mile."

"Oh, shit," Eli groaned. "Are we supposed to walk that far today?"

"We are," Holt told the pathetic killer he had hired. "And we will."

"I don't think I can make it, Mr. Holt."

Holt turned on Eli. "Oh, you'll make it even if you have to crawl on your hands and knees!"

Tears flowed down Eli's sunken cheeks, and Holt wanted to beat the sorry bastard to death with his fists, but he didn't. "People are watching us, Eli. Let's lift our heads high and get moving."

Eli stood swaying, ready to faint. After a moment, Holt grabbed the man by the arm and pulled him forward. "We're going to make it to my wagon, horses, and mules," Holt vowed. "And then we're going to drive the team back into Salt Lake City and see a real doctor, then rest and recover for a week or two."

"It might take me longer than that, Mr. Holt."

"We haven't got any longer, Eli. We'll rest and recuperate for a week or two, and then we're going to recapture Joe Moss and Fiona."

Eli turned to stare at the giant with disbelief. "Mr. Holt, those two are gone just the same as our reward money!"

"Not by a long stretch they're not."

Eli looked ready to bawl. "But we don't have any idea which way they went!"

"I was told they walked to the east and the mountains," Holt replied. "But that's only to trick us. They'll be headed for the Humboldt River and that's where we'll meet and capture them."

"You really think so?"

"I know so because they won't stop until they get their little girl back from the nuns in Virginia City." Holt snorted in anger. "Now let's show some backbone and start walking with our heads held high!"

"I'll try. How far did you say that they left your buckboard and belongings?"

"They told me one mile."

"That's a long, long ways to walk feelin' the way I do."

"We can do it, Eli. Now don't let them know how bad we feel and let's go!"

"Yes, sir," Eli said, scrubbing away his tears and putting one foot in front of the other.

The sun was high and hot. They had no water and both were weak from blood loss. But with Holt steadying Eli by holding his arm, the two men slowly walked out of Perdition into the shimmering heat of the desert. Holt knew that, if Ferris had lied, they wouldn't have the strength to come back to Perdition and they would collapse and die a mile . . . maybe even two into the desert.

It seemed like days, yet was only a tortured hour or so, when Holt lifted his head and squinted into the heat waves. "There," he croaked. "Eli, do you see the buckboard and the livestock waitin' for us out there?"

Eli was staggering, semidelirious, and just about out on his feet. He barely had the strength to lift his arm and shield his eyes. "Yeah, I see 'em now. How far away do you say we still have to walk?"

"Only a few hundred yards," Holt lied. He was sure that the Jack Mormons had left his wagon and team more than a mile from their miserable settlement. But no matter, they were going to make it.

When they finally reached the buckboard, Holt's good team of Missouri mules was braying fitfully because they were so thirsty. And the extra two horses that the Jack Mormons had left tied to the buckboard were clearly suffering for lack of water.

"Eli, we need to drain what water is left from those shot-up water barrels up in the buckboard, and then we have to water our stock, or they're going to die on us right where they stand in the next hour or two."

"Can we drink our fill first?" Eli managed to ask.

"Sure! But then we have to water the mules and horses before we lose them in this heat and dust. Once they're watered and grained out of the sacks I've got in the buckboard, we're going to drive this buckboard around this big salt lake and back east."

"Mr. Holt, do we really have to go back among them hard Mormon people?" Eli whined.

"Yes," Holt said without hesitation. "We need their help, and I still have some cash that I hid in the buckboard. We'll do all right, Eli, so buck up and don't give up. After we're rested and feeling better, we'll go catch Joe Moss and his wife and then everything will be fine. In a month, we'll both be wealthy men. We'll drink good whiskey and laugh while Joe and Fiona swing from a mining scaffold or a tree."

"I'd sure like it to work out thataway," Eli said, dredging up a hopeful smile. "I damn well surely would! After all we've gone through lately, we finally deserve some good fortune for a change."

"That we do," Holt assured the man he intended to murder just before arriving at the Comstock Lode, "that we do!"

Holt handled the heavy oaken water barrels because Eli was too weak to do the job. They had a tin bucket, and they used it to water the mules and the horses after drinking their own fill. All the animals were so thirsty they could have drunk a river, and they were hard to control.

"They're still thirsty, but they'll get by for a day, so now we give 'em grain," Holt said, filling buckets of it for his precious livestock.

"Can't we just make camp here for tonight?" Eli asked. "I'm not sure I can go on."

"I'd like nothing better than to make camp right here," Holt replied. "But I wouldn't be surprised if those men from Perdition were spying on us. I don't want them to know where we're heading, so we'll wait until dark and then get under way. With luck, we should be at the outskirts of Salt Lake City by tomorrow morning at daybreak."

"What'll we do then?"

"I don't know yet," Holt answered. "We'll just find a prosperous little Mormon farm on the outskirts of Salt Lake and take it over for a few days."

Eli frowned, trying to understand what the big man was saying to him. "You mean . . ."

"I mean we're desperate men and we'll do what we have to do."

"Sure," Eli said, not sounding sure at all. "But we don't have to hurt Mormon farm people. We'll just pay 'em to stay at their place and get to feeling better for a spell."

"That's the idea, all right."

"No killin' 'em, Mr. Holt."

The big man looked at Eli with cold eyes. "Are you suddenly going soft on me?"

"No, sir! I think we were lucky to get out of Perdition without getting our necks stretched, and I don't want to get back into that situation again with these Mormons. Not ever again."

"Relax," Holt assured the frightened man. "We'll pay for our board and keep and for that of my animals. No trouble. These farmers are always short of cash, and it'll be easy to find a place to rest up and get to feeling better. We'll get some good home cookin' from a Mormon woman. How's that sound?"

"It sounds mighty good, Mr. Holt. Mighty good!"

"I think so, too," Holt said, thinking about whether he was going to pay a Mormon family of hardworking farmers in cash . . . or in bullets.

✢ 19 ✢

Ransom Holt and Eli Brown did manage to find an isolated Mormon farm, and the young couple who owned it was desperate for cash. For thirty dollars, the Kendricks agreed to keep Holt and Eli until they were strong enough to travel. So they, along with their mules and horses, were put up in a hay barn and all were fed well, until Ransom Holt decided that they had spent enough time recovering.

"We need to leave here tomorrow and head west for the Ruby Mountains," he told Eli. "The only way to cross the desert is to reach the headwaters of the Humboldt River and follow it west across Nevada."

"And that's where you reckon that we'll find Joe Moss and his wife?" Eli asked, highly skeptical of the plan and really not feeling fit yet for a hard, dangerous desert journey.

"Yes," Holt said. "I'm going to offer Farmer Kendrick our buckboard in return for fresh food supplies and our keep while we've rested here in their hay barn."

"What about those four good Missouri mules?"

"We'll trade the mules later for more supplies and ride our two saddle horses."

"But I thought that Mr. Kendrick and you made a deal for thirty dollars."

"We did," Holt admitted, "but I decided I want to keep our cash and get rid of the buckboard, so that's what I'll tell him that he's going to have to accept in payment."

"What if he doesn't want to take the buckboard and demands the cash you promised him and his wife?"

Holt folded his massive arms across his chest and said, "Then, unfortunately, I'll have to deal harshly with Farmer Kendrick."

Eli shook his head. "Now wait just a minute, Mr. Holt. You promised me that no harm would come to any Mormons hereabouts. We barely got off with our lives in Perdition. We probably wouldn't be so lucky to do the same here."

"Eli, you worry way too damned much. This is my business and I'll handle things my way."

"But—"

"No more!"

Highly troubled and somewhat confused, Eli walked out of the barn and out into the farmer's corn and hay fields. This was good farming country, and in the distance he could see an endless sea of green patches where the industrious Mormon families had carved out hundreds of prosperous farms along the western foothills of the Wasatch Range. In just the week that he'd been recovering in the barn and eating good home cooking, Eli had come to see that being a Mormon farmer wasn't such a bad life as he might have imagined.

Not bad at all. Mr. and Mrs. Kendrick had a fine cabin, a good, weather-tight hay barn, and about two hundred acres of crops ripening in the field. They owned two plow horses, three milk cows, five hogs, and one stupid sheep. Their green hay fields were ready to be cut and stacked in the barn's loft, and Mr. Kendrick was splitting cords of wood for the coming winter weather.

As far as Eli could tell, the small Kendrick family was all about work and prayer. They were young and expecting their first child in only a few months. They were also good, decent, God-fearing folks who earned their daily bread by the sweat of their brows. And more important, Mrs. Kendrick had gone out of her way to help him and Mr. Holt recover from their terrible whippings. Not once had either of the Kendricks asked what he and Holt had done to deserve such severe punishment. Eli was more than a little grateful for their respect and courtesy.

Yes, sir, Eli thought, if he had been fortunate enough to be born into a family like the Kendricks, life might have been a little dull and monotonous, but it would have been safe and satisfying. And that was why Eli didn't want any harm to come to this good family over the promises that had been made between Mr. Kendrick and Mr. Holt.

No, sir! Eli had seen the two big men shake hands on the terms of their stay and recovery, and a deal was a deal.

"Eli?"

He turned. "Huh?"

Holt said, "Pack our saddlebags because we're leaving real soon."

Holt left then and went to the farmer's log cabin. He wasn't there very long and when he returned, Eli asked, "Did you and Mr. Kendrick come to a fair arrangement?"

"We sure did."

Eli knew he should let this go, but he just could not. "So Mr. Kendrick accepted your buckboard instead of the money you promised?"

"Uh . . . he didn't want the buckboard so I made other arrangements."

"What kind of 'arrangements' are you talking about?"

"Eli, just do as I say and get our horses saddled and the mules hitched to my buckboard. We're leaving right away."

"But . . . what did you do? Pay him the money?"

Ransom Holt's cheeks flushed with anger and he grew impatient. "I don't owe you any explanations, dammit! I told you that Mr. Kendrick and I worked out a deal," Holt snapped. "Now, dammit, do as I say! Oh, and toss some hay and about ten sacks of grain into the buckboard. I'll saddle our horses and get our bedrolls together."

Eli stared at the silent Kendrick house, and then he went to hitch their four good Missouri mules to the buckboard.

About fifteen minutes later he had the mules hitched, and all that time he'd been glancing at the cabin, expecting the Kendrick couple to at least see him and Holt off with a good-bye. But there wasn't a sound from the cabin, and Eli began to get a real bad feeling inside.

Finished with the harnessing, he headed to the cabin, for he especially wanted to thank Mrs. Kendrick for her kindness during his recovery and her delicious cooking.

"Hello the cabin? Mr. Kendrick? Mrs. Kendrick?"

"Hey!"

Eli pivoted to see Holt hurrying out of the barn toward him. "What are you doing?"

"I just wanted to say good-bye to those good folks."

"To hell with those farmers!" Holt ordered. "Climb up on that buckboard and let's go!"

Eli Brown was suddenly wishing for his Sharps rifle, which the Perdition Mormons had kept for themselves. Failing that, he was wishing for a loaded pistol on his hip.

"Mr. Holt, what happened in that cabin when you went in to offer the buckboard instead of cash?"

"Nothing you need to know about."

Eli suddenly understood that Mr. Kendrick had been hurt and maybe killed in that cabin by Holt. And then he realized that Mrs. Kendrick, big with child, might just have suffered the same cruel fate.

Ransom Holt was wearing a Colt on his hip. Eli went to the buckboard and saw a rifle that hadn't belonged to either one of them.

It's Mr. Kendrick's rifle, I'll bet!

With a pain akin to the lash of a bullwhip, Eli knew with dead certainty that Holt had done the Kendrick husband and wife a terrible, perhaps even deadly, wrong when he'd gone to their cabin.

Eli picked up the rifle, making sure that it was loaded and ready to fire. Then he turned toward Ransom Holt, who was holding the saddle horses and asked, "How did you come by taking their rifle?"

Holt's wide, handsome face froze for an instant, then broke into a wide, innocent smile. "Why, I *bought* that rifle! We're going to need it in Paiute country."

"You bought it?"

"Sure did. Mr. Kendrick said he could buy another, and I paid him ten dollars for the rifle."

"Good deal," Eli said, mind spinning. "I think I'll go and say good-bye to them."

Holt's smile slipped away. "Maybe you really, really shouldn't."

"Maybe I gotta."

Eli took the rifle and headed toward the cabin. When he reached the door, he knocked.

"Eli? Eli, get back here and get up on that buckboard!"

But Eli wouldn't turn away from the door to the cabin. He knocked hard and then called, "Mrs. Kendrick? Are you all right in there?"

"Eli! Get in the buckboard!"

Eli placed a hand on the doorknob and turned it. He eased the door wide open. "Mr. Kendrick? Mrs. Kendrick?"

The young farming couple was lying side by side on the floor and it was obvious that they had been beaten unconscious. The room was in a shambles, telling Eli that the pair had at least put up a good fight. But Ransom Holt was too big and strong to whip, and so they'd ended up losing a bad, bad fight.

"Holt," Eli swore, turning in the doorway toward the big man, "you dirty, low-down sonofabitch!"

The first bullet from Holt's revolver hit Eli high in the chest and passed through his right lung. He staggered back into the cabin a step. The second bullet struck him a foot lower, in the gut just over his belt buckle, and would have bought Eli a painful and slow death.

But the first bullet was fatal and Eli Brown was gone even before he struck the cabin's floor.

"Stupid bastard," Holt said, going into the cabin and prying the rifle out of Eli's twitching fingers. "These Mormon farmers will live. But you damn sure won't."

Then Holt shot Eli in the back of his head for good measure, and left the Mormon farm driving his buckboard and leading the two good saddle horses along behind.

He was sorry to have had to kill Eli Brown because the man was a crack rifle shot and it was probably insane to go into the desert alone. There would be Paiutes to worry about, but Ransom Holt thought he could trade the four Missouri mules for his safe passage. The thing of it was, he was sure that he would catch up to and capture

Joe and Fiona Moss and then get all the Comstock Lode bounty.

Yes, having to kill Eli was unfortunate, but Holt still felt like he was holding a winning hand in this deadly game.

✦ 20 ✦

IT WAS WITH more than a small measure of reluctance that Joe and Fiona dropped down out of the Wasatch Mountains and started into the hot desert. With Joe walking most of the time and Fiona riding the strawberry roan, they passed a few miles south of the Great Salt Lake, and headed due west across the seemingly endless ocean of alkali and salt flats. Fortunately, they were able to find and buy water from a freighter transporting salt to the Mormons.

"Any more water up ahead for a ways?" Joe asked the friendly mule skinner.

"There is, but you'll have to travel a good twenty miles to get to the first spring. You'll see my tracks leadin' to 'er."

"What about after that?"

"I wouldn't know," the freighter admitted. "I just go out there to that spring, where I dig up salt and pack it into this wagon. It's hard, mean work. Salt and alkali gets into your eyes and every crack in your body and it burns like sulfur. You and that little woman going into Nevada?"

"We may," Joe answered, not taking the chance that

Holt or Eli would come across this man and learn of their destination.

"Well, I wish you luck," the freighter called as he released the wagon brake and started rolling eastward. "That's a terrible, ugly land out there all the way to the Sierra Nevada Range."

"Not quite," Joe said. "There's the Ruby Mountains, which are green with good hunting and water."

"Yep, there are the Rubys," the freighter yelled over his shoulder. "If you live to reach 'em!"

Fiona looked at Joe with worry. "You think we can get there?"

"We can and we will, darlin'. And once we get to the Rubys and let your horse eat grass for a day or two and rest ourselves a mite, then we'll push on to the Humboldt River and then follow tracks as wide as those left by a rail line. They'll lead us straight across the desert to Reno."

"Do you think that we'll have a run-in with Paiutes?"

Joe wanted to tell her that was unlikely so his wife wouldn't fret, but that would be a deception. "I'm afraid that I'd almost bet on it. But maybe we can trade 'em somethin' for safe passage."

"What do we have to trade that Paiutes would value?"

"I been thinkin' on that," Joe told her. "And I can't think of a thing that they'd want from us save our weapons and that horse you're ridin'."

"Oh, no! Please not this horse. And not our sweet little pack burro either. I could walk. I'm getting a lot stronger, Joe."

"I know that," he said, "but I don't want you to walk."

"Then what?"

Joe patted the wooden handle of his tomahawk. "Could be those Paiutes might like my 'hawk. It's a prize, ya know."

"But it's very special to you."

"Sure it is, but I can barter for another when we return with Jessica and go back into the high mountains. The main thing is just survivin' this desert and its unfriendly Injuns."

Fiona nodded in agreement. "I'm very glad that you won't trade this roan horse or our little burro away, Joe. Not because I couldn't walk all the way to Virginia City, but because I've heard that the Paiutes are very hard on their horses and burros and eventually eat them."

"That is true. They treat 'em like the Apache and other desert Indians and that ain't kindly."

"Both of our animals are far too nice and deserving to ever be roasted over a fire."

"I reckon."

"We'll make it, Joe. We've come so far and it's been so hard that I just know that we'll somehow get Jessica and then get through all this ugliness and killing."

"I reckon we will, Fiona."

"I love you, Joe."

"I . . . I love ya, too, Fiona, darlin of mine."

Joe had once before gone to the Sierra Nevada Mountains, but then he'd traveled with other mountain men and they'd circled to the north of the Great Salt Lake and then crossed these vast salt and alkali flats. That was said to be the preferred way for a man to cross this desert hell. But now they were striking out on a little-used dirt track southwest of the Great Salt Lake, and Joe figured that they would meet very few travelers and hopefully even fewer Paiutes. This was a time of the full moon, and normally a fella might have slept in the daytime and traveled in the night when it was cooler. But sleeping by day was impossible out here on the flats where even the hardy sagebrush was sparse and runty. There were almost no rocks or arroyos to hide in or find shade or shelter in.

The most compelling issue was the availability of water. A man or a horse might go three days and nights without water in the heat of a desert, but then he was cooked. That told Joe that they had to find at least one spring or source of drinking water on the way to the Ruby Mountains. And if they didn't . . . well, he had been told that dying of thirst was a real hard and ugly way to go, and he sure didn't want that to happen to Fiona.

For the next few days, they made better-than-expected time. The wind didn't blow and there were still faint wagon tracks to follow westward. They continued across a dead lake floor, and each footstep crushed an inch or two of powdery salt and alkali, which didn't make walking any easier. But for a mile or two at a stretch, the ground was firm and easier to tread. Fiona was a trouper, and she never complained as they kept moving from dawn to dusk with only a few short rest stops.

"I reckon we're halfway to the Rubys," Joe said as they made another cold, fireless camp.

"Joe, your feet are bleeding from blisters!"

"It's the salt that gets into these boots," Joe told her. "Your feet sweat and the salt mixes with it and rubs the flesh raw."

"And look at your poor ankles!" Fiona said, pulling up his pants a little and staring at the inflamed skin. "You must be in terrible pain!"

"I'll live through it," he told her. "The shackles we wore opened up the flesh, and the salt gets into it and makes it burn and fester."

Fiona spoke in a way that brooked no argument. "Tomorrow you are riding the strawberry and I'm walking."

"Fiona, I can't—"

"They'll be no more talk about it," she said. "Tomorrow you ride and I walk. How is our water holding out?"

"Almost gone. I gave the horse and burro half of one canteen tonight, and they're both still suffering. We got half of the other canteen left for ourselves."

Fiona understood their predicament and said, "Then we *have* to find water tomorrow."

Joe looked toward the setting sun. "We do," he admitted. "We surely do. Fiona, I think we ought to rest a few hours and then strike out and travel through the night. I've been studyin' the lay of this hard land and what we're doin' right now is crossing an old dry lake bed. But just up ahead maybe five or six miles is the shoreline of the lake bed and then we're into the sagebrush flats. And I see some low hills off to the north a little ways. To me, they look as if they hold the promise of water."

"Do we dare go out of our way even a mile to look?"

"I don't think we have any choice," Joe said. "We just got to get some water by this time tomorrow."

"I know," she said. "My throat is so dry that I couldn't spit if my life depended upon it."

"We'll head for those foothills. If I see the tracks of wild mustangs or deer, then I'll know that there has to be a spring up in there and we'll damn sure find good water."

Fiona took Joe's hand. "Tomorrow is pretty much going to decide if we make it across here alive, isn't that true?"

"It is," Joe confessed. "And if we don't . . . well, I'm gonna feel real bad about this because we've come too far to turn back."

"I believe in you, Joe. I believe you will find us water tomorrow, but I'll also be praying to God that he guides us out of this hell and leads us to the Humboldt River."

"You go ahead and do that," Joe told her. "Might not help, but it sure can't hurt."

"That's the way I see it, too," Fiona said.

Joe dozed off, and Fiona awakened him when the stars

were all shining and the Big Dipper showed them where north was so they could adjust and keep going straight west.

The strawberry roan's eyes had sunk deep into its sockets, and the horse had lost a hundred pounds or more since they'd found him. The burro was handling the lack of water a little better, and Joe had lightened its pack down to less than fifty pounds. The tough little animal wasn't a complainer; it just kept its big head down low and kept plodding forward.

"Horse shit!" Joe exclaimed about three o'clock in the morning in the light of the moon. "These are wild mustang droppings and tracks leading into those northern foothills."

"Then?"

"Then I expect they have a secret water hole," Joe said, feeling hope flood through his weary and pain-racked body. "The water hole won't be clean, Fiona. Far, far from it. It'll have horse shit and bird shit and all kinds of dead insects, lizards, and crap floatin' in that water. It'll be muddy and probably taste awful . . . but it'll be safe to drink or the wild horses wouldn't touch it."

"I don't care what it tastes like," she told him. "If we find water, then we'll be saved."

"For a few days at least."

Joe glanced up at the moon and stars, and then he jumped off the roan and hoisted Fiona into the saddle. "I'll need to be on foot to follow the mustang tracks," he said, although he could have easily followed them from horseback. "You ride now."

"But your feet are in terrible shape, Joe. And you've only ridden a few hours!"

"It was long enough and my feet feel a whole lot better."

Joe collected the Spencer rifle and made sure that it was ready to fire. He had two six-shot pistols in his waistband

and he was thinking that, if the mustangs knew of this water hole, so would the Paiutes, who had survived in this land for centuries.

"Keep up with me," he said, looking back over his shoulder at his wife on the strawberry. "And keep the burro tethered to that saddle horn. He might try to stampede ahead when he gets his first whiff of water."

"I will."

Joe followed the mustang tracks with hope growing in his chest. After less than a mile of hiking into the foothills, the strawberry roan and the burro both caught the scent of water, and they nearly knocked him over as they hurried forward.

"Stay back of me!" Joe called. "There could be Indians up ahead!"

But Fiona was in too weakened a state to be able to control either animal as the pair charged over a low hill and down toward a large desert watering hole.

Two Paiutes were camping at the water hole, and they'd heard the onrushing Joe, Fiona, and their animals. The had their weapons ready to fire, but they shot too quickly, missing Fiona just as Joe topped the hill and charged down toward the Indians, whooping and hollering like the Man Killer of his storied youth.

The Indians panicked. Joe threw the Spencer to his shoulder. When he fired, the first Paiute was knocked spinning into the shallow and muddy water hole. The remaining Paiute threw down his empty rifle and vanished into the night.

"Damn!" Joe cried.

"What do we do now?" Fiona called, her strawberry roan already standing in the water hole along with the burro while both animals drank the muddy water.

"Let the beasts drink a minute or two longer and then get 'em out of there or they'll bust their bellies."

Joe thought about racing after the Paiute that had escaped, but he knew he'd never catch the Indian. He was too weak and his feet were in too bad a shape to run.

And besides that, the Paiute he'd shot wasn't dead yet. Joe saw the man struggle to crawl out of the water hole and one of his arms was dangling.

I missed his body and hit him in the arm.

Joe skidded to the edge of the water and pointed his pistol down at the Indian struggling to climb out of the slippery water hole. For a moment their dark eyes, each burnished by moonlight, locked.

Then Joe kicked the Indian in the head and knocked him out cold. Before the Paiute could drown, Joe dragged him up to the muddy bank and tied him hand and foot.

"What are you doing!" Fiona cried.

"I'm buyin' us a little edge in this game," Joe gritted. "Now we got something even better'n my 'hawk to trade the Paiutes for safe passage across the rest of this hell."

But Fiona wasn't really listening. She was throwing herself off the strawberry roan into the muddy water hole and gulping down mouthfuls of the foul-tasting but life-giving water.

At daybreak, the Paiute awoke, and immediately tried to get up and run away. When he discovered that he was tied hand and foot and trapped, he threw back his head and began to howl.

"Is he going to bring others down on us?" Fiona asked anxiously.

"He might," Joe said, "but it's more likely that his friend that got away last night will find the rest and they'll come."

Fiona shook her head. "So we're going to be surrounded by Indians and they'll be looking for revenge."

"I expect that is true," Joe agreed.

"What do we do now?"

Joe had been soaking his poor blistered feet in the mud, and now he washed them off and pulled on his boots. "Fiona," he said, "we can either make a stand here where we got water, or we can make a run for the Rubys hopin' that the one that got away has a long distance to go to get to his friends."

Fiona thought about that for a moment while she looked all around at the water hole. It was down in a shallow bowl, and even she knew that it would be impossible to defend against more than half a dozen Paiutes. "I want to make a run for it, Joe."

"So do I," he said. "So now that we've all drunk every bit of water our bellies can hold, let's move out."

"What about the Paiute? I tried to mend his arm and he tried to bite me."

"He's young and he's scared," Joe told her. "And besides that, his wound ain't nothin' but a scratch. We'll take him along and hope for the best."

"You said he could be our ticket out of this hell," Fiona said. "That we could trade him for safe passage."

"That's right. Let's just hope he's important to his tribe and they think he's worth tradin' for."

"Yes, let's."

Joe tightened the cinch on the strawberry roan and helped Fiona back into the saddle. They'd all drunk as much of the water as they could hold, and immediately gotten the shits for their trouble. But that would pass. The canteens were full and it was time to leave.

Joe cut the Paiute's ankle bonds with his hunting knife, and then put a noose around the young warrior's neck. He used the knife blade to point to the west where they would go.

The Paiute understood, but he spat at Joe and then cursed him. Joe jabbed the Paiute in his bare ass with the point of the hunting knife, and the young warrior yelped and howled in pain.

"Move!" Joe ordered, holding the knife up and making it clear that he would keep sticking the Indian until he did as ordered.

The Paiute cussed him out again. He was a thin, dirty fellow and not much taller than Fiona. His long, black hair was tied back in a braid and his black eyes blazed with hatred.

"I don't expect you to like me seein' as how I shot you. But I didn't do much harm and you'll come out of this alive . . . if we do. Now move!"

The young Paiute warrior raised his chin in defiance. Joe jabbed him again in the ass with the sharp point of his knife. This time the Paiute didn't yell, and he started forward. They climbed out of the water hole bowl, and Joe glanced back wondering if he was doing the wrong thing by making a run for the Rubys.

"Fiona, make 'em trot!"

Fiona kicked the strawberry into a trot, and the poor little burro had to really work to keep up with the horse. Joe jabbed the Paiute into a jog and they hurried westward.

He just hoped to hell they could reach the Rubys before the Paiutes caught up with them.

✢ 21 ✢

JOE MOSS WAS a powerful man, and one who had learned to endure the kind of intense pain and hardships that would have broken most men. But now, with the Ruby Mountains plainly in sight, he just could not take another faltering step.

"Hold up," he called to Fiona on the strawberry roan. "I . . . I can't walk any farther today."

"It's your feet?"

"Yeah," Joe said, "they're infected and so swollen up I couldn't get my boots off last night."

Fiona jumped down from the strawberry roan and, ignoring their young Paiute captive, she said, "Sit down, Joe. I'm going to take those boots off and then we'll bathe your feet and doctor them as best we can out here in the desert. After that, you're going to ride the rest of the way to the Rubys and I'll lead the burro and our young Indian captive."

Joe wanted to protest, but he knew that was stupid. Both of his feet had gone way beyond the point of his painful blisters. They were burning and he was, too, feeling woozy and feverish.

Joe unholstered his gun and pointed it at their captive. "Just so you don't think about tryin' to escape," he warned.

"He won't try," Fiona told Joe. "His hands are still tied behind his back."

"Oh, he'll run if he gets the chance," Joe said. "And I'll bet he's faster'n I am even with those hands tied."

"Let's get those boots off," Fiona said, concern written all over her face. "I'm really worried about your feet."

"They'll probably be all right."

"We'll see about that," Fiona said. "Now lean back and give me your boot and I'll try to pull it off."

Fiona pulled and pulled while Joe tried not to yelp. When Fiona couldn't pull the damned boot off, she tried the other with the same results. Looking up at Joe, she said, "Your feet are so swollen up that we'll have to cut the boots off in order to do the doctoring."

"Maybe we should just leave them on for now," Joe suggested. "We'll be up to the Ruby Mountains and finally outa this desert by midnight. Once we get into the mountains, we can rest up a day or two and I'll soak my feet in some icy stream."

"But if your feet are so infected that they're starting to poison your blood, we really should tend to them right now."

"Help me up on the roan," Joe said. "And let's get to the mountains. I got a strong hunch that the Paiutes are closing on our back trail. If we get to the mountains, we can defend ourselves better."

Fiona nodded with understanding. "All right, Joe. If that's what you think is best."

"It is," Joe said. "Now help me get onto that strawberry roan."

Once Joe was mounted, he took the rope that was tied around the Paiute's neck and wrapped the other end around his saddle horn. Then he pointed to the mountains and kicked his horse in the ribs.

If the young Paiute had any intention of slowing their progress to help his friends, they were instantly dispelled as he was abruptly jerked forward by the roan. With the noose tight around his neck, he had no choice but to follow along at a trot. Fiona picked up the burro's lead rope and followed as best she could.

In the late afternoon, less than an hour before sundown, Joe, now feeling dizzy with fever, turned and tried to see if he could spot Paiutes. He was afraid that he would not be able to do much in the way of fighting them if the negotiations he had hoped for failed.

"Do you see them coming?" Fiona asked.

Joe closed one eye because he was seeing double. "Yeah," he said at last. "I think that I do."

"Where!"

Joe pointed. "Look out into the desert and just to the east of that little rocky knoll and that's where you'll see something moving. I think that's our Paiutes."

Fiona shaded her eyes for a moment and then gasped. "Oh, Joe, they are on ponies and closing fast on us!"

"We can make the mountains and find a good place to hole up and fight if we have to. My eyes are givin' me a bit of trouble, Fiona. How many can you count?"

"About ten," she said after a moment.

"Ten," Joe said to himself. "That's more'n I was hopin' would follow, but we can still handle 'em."

"Can we?"

"We don't have any choice. Ain't no cavalry out here and no whites that would care to help us if they heard rifle shots."

"Let's go!" Fiona urged.

Their captive looked back and smiled. Then, before Joe or Fiona could stop him, he let out a high-pitched scream that probably carried for miles in the clear, hot air.

"Shut up!" Joe yelled, yanking out his pistol and trying to focus on the Paiute. "You yell again and I'll kill ya!"

The young Paiute didn't yell, but he didn't stop smiling either.

"Let's push it," Fiona pleaded. "Those mountains up ahead are probably farther away than they look."

"They always are," Joe agreed.

For the next five hours and well into the night, they pushed themselves to their physical limits. They were low on water and food, so they were weak. Fiona was staggering when they finally got up into the tall pine trees and then continued along a game trail until they reached a little stream and meadow.

"Can't we stop right here, Joe?"

Joe was slipping in and out of consciousness and his fever was raging.

"Joe! Joe, can we stop here?"

He roused himself with all his willpower and looked around at the moonlit meadow, and then he saw the rushing stream. "Let's follow it a little higher, Fiona. We got to find a spot where it goes through a narrow place with rocks. That's where we can hole up and make our best stand."

Fiona nodded and led the way forward. Joe gripped his saddle horn with both fists and tried to keep his eye on their Paiute captive. Soon, they did pass through the moonlit meadow and into rocks. The sound of the water was loud and Joe knew that, unlike the hidden mustang water hole from which they'd last drunk their fill, this water would be clear and sweet.

"This is a good enough place for us to fight!" Joe called, swaying precariously in his saddle. "Let's all drink and then hole up in those big rocks."

"Will the Paiutes attack us in the night?"

"I don't think so," Joe said, tumbling out of the saddle and crawling to the stream to drink. "I . . . I don't think so."

Joe drank deeply, and then he swiveled around and shoved his booted feet into the stream and pulled up his pants so that the water poured into his boot tops and filled them. Moments later, his feet didn't burn so bad, and he looked up at the stars, thinking maybe he'd live through this night.

"Fiona!"

She was at his side, and when she touched his brow she softly began to cry. "Joe, you're on fire."

"Help me get all the way into that stream."

"But the water is so cold and the night air up here is chilly."

"That's right," he moaned. "That's what I need right now."

Fiona dragged Joe into the rushing stream, and the feeling of the icy mountain water pouring over his body was pure pleasure.

"Get our Indian tied hand and foot and back under the rocks along with our horse and burro," Joe ordered. "Unload our packs and get everything back in and under those big rocks and make sure that all the weapons are loaded. But don't unsaddle the strawberry roan in case everything goes to hell and you need to get on that horse and make a run for the Humboldt River."

"I won't leave you here!"

"Ain't no use in both of us dyin' if you can live, Fiona. Now just let me lie here a little longer and I'll be feelin' a mite better."

Fiona didn't look like she believed Joe, but she knew that the Paiutes were very close now, so she did as he instructed. It took her less than twenty minutes to take care of the animals and tie the Paiute securely. He tried to kick and knock her down, then get away, but she hit him with the barrel of the pistol just hard enough to get him to behave.

"All right, Joe," she said, returning to the stream. "Everything is taken care of like you wanted."

"Good woman," he said, rousing himself. "Now help me back under the rocks and we just wait and see what them Indians want to do . . . fight or do tradin' talk."

Joe awoke with light peeking through the cracks of the big rocks and Fiona shaking his shoulder. "Joe, they're standing out there across from the stream and it looks like they want to talk."

Joe felt like he was climbing out of a tunnel. "Talk? Who?"

"The Paiutes that have been chasing us!"

"My fever is high," Joe confessed. "You might have to do the palaverin' yourself."

"But . . . but I can't do that! I don't speak Paiute!"

"Make sign," Joe told her. "Tell 'em we'll trade their young warrior for safe passage to the Humboldt River. Tell 'em we need to stay here a week or so until I get strong enough to travel. And ask 'em if they have any medicine for my feet. And Fiona?"

"Yes?"

"Be sure to tell them that my Indian name is Man Killer."

"I'll do that. Should I have a gun in my hand when I go out there to talk?"

"Do the Paiutes have their guns in their hands?"

"Yes."

"Then you take my pistols . . . both of 'em, and make sure they are loaded and ready to fire. And you go out and make us a deal. Tell them that Man Killer is waiting to hear what they say. But we'll take any deal so long as we can keep our weapons, the horse, and the burro, and they get their friend."

Joe wanted to say more, but his world started spinning and he closed his eyes. Darkness came swiftly.

Fiona had spent all morning trying to make her demands known to the Indians who stood on the other side of the Ruby Mountains stream. When the Paiutes learned that Man Killer was guarding their warrior, they grew very serious and started to talk to Fiona much more respectfully. Over and over and over, she had used crude sign language and words to convey her wishes. Fortunately, two of the older Paiutes knew some English, but unfortunately, they obviously liked to dicker and deal.

At noon, when Fiona was nearly wild with worry about Joe's infected feet and what was going to happen to them, it seemed like she had a breakthrough in the discussion. Even better, it turned out that one of the two older Indians who spoke broken English was a Paiute medicine man.

"Come over here," Fiona said, pointing to the medicine man and urging him to wade across the cold stream. "Husband very sick. Man Killer very sick with bad feet!"

Fiona pointed to her feet, and then she rolled her eyes up in her head and acted woozy. The Paiute understood and nodded with concern. At that point, Fiona knew that once these people understood that Man Killer could not fight, she was very vulnerable to being killed. But the old medicine man came across the stream by himself, and soon they were cutting off Joe's boots and staring at Joe's badly infected feet.

Fiona was not a nurse nor had she done a lot of doctoring, but she had seen wounds become infected with gangrene and she knew what that smelled and looked like. Joe's feet were almost, but not quite, gangrenous.

"My husband needs strong Paiute medicine," she said repeatedly.

The medicine man went over to the captive and inspected the young man's arm. He frowned, and then he whirled and marched back across the stream to get his medicines. At that point, Fiona thought the old Paiute might tell his companions to attack and kill the helpless white man with bad feet and enslave his woman. Fiona gripped her pistols tightly and vowed to fight to the death, if necessary. She would never again allow herself to be taken captive by red man or white.

But the medicine man returned with his herbs, and soon he had a little fire going and was boiling all his medicines and stream water in a pottery jug. Then he made poultices out of plant leaves and moss from the streambed and wrapped Joe's badly infected feet.

"Make good medicine," the old Paiute proclaimed, thumping his bony chest. "Me good medicine man!"

Fiona bowed her head with respect, pistols still in her hands. "Yes, you are a good medicine man . . . I hope."

The Paiutes camped for two days on the other side of the beautiful mountain stream. They seemed to be in no particular hurry to leave or go about any other business. Fiona had made it very clear that only the medicine man was to cross to her side of the stream and join her under the big rocks to make his medicine.

Joe's fever broke and his vision became clear again. When he understood what was going on, he sat up and thanked the medicine man with extravagant praise. Then he stated that he wanted to trade safe passage for them to the

Humboldt River and in return he would let their captive young Paiute go free.

And so began the bargaining all over again. It lasted another two days, and ended only when Joe pulled his tomahawk from his pack and two scalps that he had secretly kept hidden from Fiona.

"Man Killer scalp Sitting Bull!" he roared, half laughing because this was totally untrue. He waved the scalps in a circle overhead and howled and chanted a few Cheyenne songs just to make it all seem true. "This other belonged to Crazy Horse!"

But the Paiutes believed him, and went wild over the tomahawk and the two scalps belonging to famous Plains Indian war chiefs. And when Joe promised to throw in a pistol along with their hostage, the deal was finally agreed on. After that, the Paiutes were grinning from ear to ear and there was no doubt that they thought Man Killer and his woman were now their good and true friends.

That night, Joe and Fiona dared to sleep for a few hours as they huddled close under the rocks. Their captive was snoring, and his elbow had been doctored by the Paiute medicine man, who pronounced that the young man's arm would fully mend.

"Do you think they'll betray and kill us after we leave these mountains and go down with them back into the desert?"

"No," Joe said. "I don't. They want my 'hawk and those two scalps real bad. I also promised to give 'em five dollars, which they can use to buy plenty of whiskey at some trading post way the hell out on the Humboldt."

"When you were unconscious with fever, they could easily have killed me, Joe."

But Joe shook his head. "They could have done those things, but from your hard looks they decided you would not only fight, but you know how to use those two pistols, and that some of them would die. When you made it clear you wanted to swap their young man for safe passage, they felt that was a good and fair trade. And when they learned I was Man Killer, with the scalps of Crazy Horse and Sitting Bull, they would have given us all their Indian ponies in trade, but I only asked for one."

"If you hadn't missed at the mustangs' water hole and you'd actually killed one or even both Indians, would we have been able to make a deal?"

"No," Joe told her. "If I'd shot quicker and straighter and killed one or both at the water hole, we'd be dead by now."

Fiona shook her head in wonder. "Sometimes, Joe, the Lord really does work in strange ways."

"I don't know if he was workin' or not when I missed killing that pair, but I'll give ya the benefit of the doubt."

"Your poor feet are looking a lot better."

"I should never have put on a dead man's boots," Joe told her. "I should have made myself a pair of moccasins like I usually wear."

Fiona leaned her head back against Joe's shoulder and looked up at the night. The stream was a constant, comforting sound.

"I like it here in the Ruby Mountains where it's cool and green and where there's sweet, cold water. I wish we could stay here, Joe."

"If you want, after we go to Virginia City and get our girl, we can come back here to live. These mountains aren't big like the Rockies or the Wasatch, but they're big enough for us to live in for the rest of our days without ever being crowded by white people."

"Maybe that would be nice," Fiona mused as she looked upward. "Maybe we should think seriously about that, Joe."

"Fine by me," he said. "But we got a lot of hard travelin' to do before we can get to Virginia City and back. And there's going to be some killin' along the way, Fiona."

"Must there be?"

"I'm afraid so. I won't leave the Comstock Lode until the last Peabody man either shakes my hand and swears to me the blood feud is over between us . . . or I kill him and it's over. Either way, I won't have people comin' after me and you anymore for a Peabody bounty."

"I understand."

"I'm glad that you do," Joe said, holding his wife close. "And if this Paiute wasn't here under the rock with us . . . well, I was thinkin' that maybe you and me could cozy up a little closer and . . ."

"Oh, Joe! You really are starting to feel better."

"I am," Joe admitted. "And I'm a-thinkin' that I'd like to have a taste of you before we go back out in the damned hot desert."

"While we're cool and clean?"

"Yep. And before the salt and alkali gets into our creases again."

Fiona listened to their captive snore for a few minutes, and then she pulled their blanket over them and one by one began to unbutton buttons.

"Oh, Joe!" she moaned a short time later. "You *are* feeling ever so much better!"

Joe grunted, and his long body convulsed with pleasure as he emptied his seed into his sweet wife.

✢ 22 ✢

THEY WERE LEAVING the Paiutes as friends, and Joe had even given the young warrior he'd shot in the arm a good, two-bladed pocketknife that he'd taken off the man who'd been killed by the sow grizzly bear.

"We may soon pass this way again," Joe told the Paiutes in sign language and broken English. "In one moon, we will bring our daughter, Jessica, to show you."

The old medicine man had prepared more poultices, and had shown Joe and Fiona how to take his medicines out of a pouch and then boil and apply them as hot as Joe could stand.

"I'll do 'er," Joe promised. "Your strong medicine has probably saved my feet and our lives. I will forever be a friend of your Ruby Mountains Paiute clan."

Joe and Fiona were ready to travel, and the Paiute pointed them toward the Humboldt River. And before leaving, the headman of the Paiutes gave Joe an eagle feather tied to a small but intricately carved red ceremonial stick and let him know that, if they were confronted by other

Paiutes, they had only to show them this sign and Joe and Fiona would be protected and allowed to pass unharmed.

And so, on a cool, windy day, they said their final good-bye and Joe helped Fiona onto her new Indian pony. The mare was small, thin, and unshod like all Indian ponies and nothing much to look at, but Joe had been assured by the Paiutes that the pony was sound and safe for anyone to ride with only a blanket and a rope through its mouth. Joe had packed their little burro, and now he wrapped the burro's lead rope around his saddle horn and mounted the strawberry roan.

"I sure hate to leave these cool mountains," Fiona said.

"Me, too," Joe agreed. "But there's no choice."

So off they rode down into the desert again, and the day grew warmer. There was no trail, but Joe Moss was a man accustomed to making his own trails, so they kept a straight line to where the Paiutes had pointed. According to the Paiutes, they should be able to reach the Humboldt River by nightfall.

"Fiona," Joe said later that afternoon with the sun beating down on their heads, "how's that little Indian pony treating you?"

"I liked the strawberry roan you're riding a lot better, and a real saddle sure is nicer than this Indian blanket."

"I'm sorry about that," Joe said, grinning. "But the pony is just too small to carry me and a heavy saddle. And anyway, look way out yonder there and you'll see what appears to be a silver ribbon."

"Is that the Humboldt River?"

"It is," Joe told her.

"Is it a *real* river, Joe? I mean like the Arkansas or the Colorado?"

"Afraid not. The Humboldt runs year-round, but it's shallow and you have to watch for quicksand. There used to be trees linin' its banks for a hundred miles across this desert, but the pilgrims all cut 'em down for axles and firewood. Used to be some beaver there, too, but we trapped 'em all out."

"What's left?"

"Just marshes and lots of birds that follow the river across this desert. Plenty of foxes and muskrats and frogs and such."

"Did you say frogs?"

"Yep."

"I *love* frog legs."

"Then you'll have 'em most every night," Joe promised. "We might even get lucky enough to hook up with a wagon train. If we do, we'll just tag along to be fed in exchange for chores."

"I would like the company of women," Fiona said wistfully. "It's been a long time since I've been around them. But . . ."

Joe saw the dark clouds of worry pass across his wife's eyes. "But what? Speak out what's botherin' ya."

Tears began to stream down Fiona's face. "Joe," she said, riding closer, "you must know what Jedediah Charles and Ike did to me at that dugout."

"Yeah, I know. But that's in the past and we won't ever talk about it again."

"But I *have* to talk about it!" Fiona slipped off her Indian pony and fell to her knees, sobbing.

Joe jumped off the strawberry roan, ignoring the pain in his mending feet, and knelt by her side in the sand and sagebrush. "Fiona, you can't let things that happened to you in the past destroy your future. *Our future.* Just put it plain out of your mind."

She looked up at him. "You're so strong, Joe. But I'm

not you. I can't just put it out of my mind. It *preys* on my mind!"

Joe enclosed her in his strong arms. "Darlin', if I let some of the things that I've done to other men or they did to me prey on my mind, why, I'd most likely go mad. So when them bad thoughts come around, I just push 'em back and think of good things. Like that stream we camped beside in the Ruby Mountains, or maybe a big elk bull that I saw standin' on a mountaintop and buglin' to the world that he was the lord of all his timberland. Or a big fish jumpin' high in the fadin' sunlight, shiny as quicksilver. Or snow geese honkin' in the sky just joyous to be headin' south for the winter. Trees turning gold in autumn. Ice on a streambed and cold, clean air swelling in your lungs. You know, good things, and when I think of them, well, all the bad things in my mind just go away."

Fiona nodded. "I'm not sure that I've seen all those beautiful things that you've just described and can use them."

Joe winked. "Then think of our beautiful girl and how we might just have added another Moss to the family two nights ago. Do think of Jessica! She needs us both to be there for her to be strong of mind, body, and spirit. She ain't never had us both there for her, but soon she will."

Joe swallowed hard. "Darlin', if you can't think of the things I described in nature, just think of our Jessica and your mind will come around to be right."

"Joe, I will."

"You started cryin' when you talked about meetin' and bein' around other women, so you musta been thinkin' that maybe you don't deserve to be with 'em given all the grief you've been handed in your life. Is that it?"

"It is."

"Don't give 'er another thought, darlin'. You're ever' bit

as good, decent, and strong as any woman, and none in this world has the right to look down on your pretty head. Not a single one!"

"But what if they learn about all the unspeakable outrages that were committed against my body?"

"They won't. The men that did that to you are dead, and I scalped 'em alive. Dead men don't tell no tales, and they're howlin' in Hell right now. What happened is done, just like seasons gone. You're startin' all over new with me and our girl. We got a fresh start as soon as we get her back from the Catholic nuns. A fresh start. I gave away my 'hawk, partly because I don't intend to do any more scalpin', and I'll only kill those who try to kill or harm us and our young'uns."

"Do you really think we can get our daughter and live out our lives in peace and happiness? Do you, Joe?"

"I believe we can," he said with conviction. "Soon as this business with Peabody is done. And there's Ransom Holt and Eli and that half-breed Johnny Redman out there somewhere that I may have yet to kill. But after those bloody sonofabitches, I think we'll find our lasting peace on this earth. I really do, Fiona."

"I sure hope so," she said, voice shaking with emotion. "We've both seen so much of the bad in this world, so much blood and death and hurting, that I sometimes wonder where the good went and if it'll ever come back to bless our lives."

"It went away when I was banned from that wagon train where I met you years ago. It happened exactly when they caught us together makin' love and drove me from their midst and then we got lost from one another for so long. But we came back together, Fiona. And this time we're not ever again goin' to be torn apart. Not ever!"

"I believe you, Joe."

"Then let me hoist you back on that ugly Paiute pony and let's get to the river and I'll see if I can gig some bullfrogs. Frog legs is startin' to sound mighty tasty to me, woman."

"You gig 'em and I'll fry 'em up fine for us, Joe!"

He helped her up on her pony, and then painfully climbed up into the saddle. Fiona was smiling again and that, as far as Joe was concerned, was all the sunshine he'd ever need in this mortal world.

From a high lookout on a mountaintop, the half-breed Johnny Redman saw the Moss pair ride out of the Ruby Mountains, and he turned to Ransom Holt. "Just like we figured."

Holt nodded and smiled. "When you look at Joe and Fiona Moss, think of money. Lots and lots of money and all that it will buy. Land, women, liquor. Whatever is your pleasure. Why, breed, you can go back to your people and be the headman! You can buy as many squaws as you please and live like a tipi king!"

Holt thought that amusing, and laughed. But Johnny Redman saw no humor in those words, and deep in his heart he knew that the road to the Comstock Lode was going to be filled with bloodshed and treachery. It was only a matter of who killed who first.

"Tipi king?" Johnny asked. "That what you said?"

"Yeah," Holt crowed. "That's what I said."

Johnny Redman watched the Moss pair as they traveled along. He wondered where Fiona had gotten the little black Indian pony. Had the pair run into Paiutes and traded with them somewhere between here and Salt Lake City? Most likely they had, which told Redman that Joe Moss was a friend of the Paiutes. That was worth remembering.

"I've been thinking about where we'll take 'em," Holt said. "And how we'll do it. Joe Moss is probably armed, and he and his woman won't go down without a fight to the death."

"But we can't let that happen," Redman said. "Because they're far more valuable to Peabody alive."

"Exactly. So we have to try to take them both alive."

"How?"

"I'm thinking on it, breed. I'm thinking on it. And you know what?"

"What?"

"There's no reason for us to take 'em down for a week or two. I mean, we know their destination is Virginia City to collect their daughter. So instead of us catching Joe and his wife right away and then having all the headache of watching over them constantly, we can just tag along a few miles behind and wait until they've crossed the desert."

"Makes sense," Redman said. "Unless they're attacked and killed by the Paiutes."

"I'd bet money that Joe has cut some kind of deal for safe passage across this desert," Holt said. "He speaks Injun and he can do sign language. So my gut tells me that they'll do just fine along the Humboldt."

"So," Redman said, "when we do decide to take them, how will we do it?"

"I'm not sure," Holt said. "But seein' as how we've got a week or two to decide, I'll be making us a plan for the capture."

"You do that," Redman told the giant. "And by the way, you never did tell me what happened to Eli."

"Aw," Holt said, "he lost his nerve and decided to go back to whatever hole he climbed out of."

"He just up and left, not caring about the Comstock reward anymore?"

"That's right," Holt said. "After he lost his brother, he wasn't the same man that I'd hired, so I was glad to have him quit. It just makes the bounty all the larger for you and me to split."

"Yeah," Redman said, watching the Moss couple as they reached the Humboldt and then disappeared down a cutback toward the water, where they would most likely spend this first night by the river.

"You're quiet a lot of the time," Holt said. "I like that fine. Eli and Dalton were always jabbering and that got on my nerves."

Redman had no comment.

"But you know something, breed? There are times like right now when I'd really like to know your thoughts."

"I was thinking about how Joe Moss and his wife got hold of that black Indian pony and wondering what kind of rifle and pistols he has and how much ammunition."

"Yeah, I was wondering about the Indian pony myself. Joe probably stole the little bastard."

"Maybe."

"I've seen you shoot that pistol and use your knife," Holt was saying, "but I'm wondering how good a rifle shot you are."

"I can hit what I aim for," Redman said without elaborating.

"Can you shoot well enough to maybe crease Joe Moss in the head and knock him out cold?"

Redman turned to look at the giant as if he were insane. "No."

"Hmmm, too bad. That would sure make things easier."

"Taking Joe Moss isn't going to be easy," Redman replied. "And it might get one or both of us killed."

"Not if we use our heads and do things right," Holt

argued. "If it was Moss all by himself, then I'd be a bit worried. But the key to taking him alive is his wife. Joe has shown us that he'll do most anything to save that skinny red-haired woman."

"Yeah," Redman said, "he has."

"So if we could sneak up into his camp after a week or so . . . you know, at night when the frogs and crickets are loud and block out all sounds of our comin', then we could grab Fiona and we'd have Joe right where we want him again . . . which is in shackles and chains."

When Johnny Redman didn't show any enthusiasm for this plan, Holt grew irritated. "Well, dammit, what do you think of that for a plan?"

Johnny didn't dare tell the giant what he really thought about him . . . or his plan to capture the Moss woman. But in time he would tell Ransom Holt a whole lot of things, none of which the giant would like to hear.

"Breed, I'm talking to you!"

"It's a plan that might work," Redman said.

"Well, it had better. And you bein' a half-breed, I expect that you could sneak up on them about any time you wanted some dark night. Couldn't you?"

"If everything was right I could," Redman said.

"Well, when the night comes when you think that everything is right, you damn sure tell me so."

"I will."

"Any other thoughts?" Holt asked, his irritation still rankling him.

"Nope."

"Then let's ride on down to the river and make our own damn camp about two miles from Moss and his woman."

Johnny Redman let the giant lead off. It was amusing how the big man wanted to know his inner thoughts. What a fool! And wouldn't he be surprised to learn that it was in Johnny Redman's mind to kill Ransom Holt so that he could collect all the Comstock bounty money for himself and his half-starved reservation people.

"THIS IS THE longest, most stinky and ugly river I have ever seen!" Fiona told Joe after they had been following the Humboldt for over a week. "How much farther does it go?"

"We're almost to where this river peters out and just sinks into the sand," Joe replied. "After the river dies, what is next is called the Humboldt Sink, and it's where a lot of good people traveling west with wagons got their hearts broken and lost everything they owned. When we get to the sink, you're going to see a lot of heartbreak."

Fiona shook her head. "To have come this far in a wagon . . . probably from St. Louis or even farther . . . and then to have to throw out everything because your animals were too weak to pull your wagons across a bad stretch of deep sand . . . that is heartbreaking."

"Yeah," Joe agreed. "As near as I remember, it's about forty miles of hell and its sands are littered with abandoned wagons, the bones of animals, and just about everything else you can imagine. When I went across five years ago, I saw pianos, beds, fine maple dressers, tools, everything and anything they could toss to lighten the load for their wagon teams."

Fiona shook her head. "I'm not looking forward to seeing all that heartache lyin' in the sand."

"And there are plenty of graves, too," Joe told her. "A lot of the folks just got sick and tired of the sand and hardship, so they gave up and died in that stretch between us and Lake Crossin'."

"But we'll be fine, won't we?"

"Yep," Joe said. "It's the cooler time of the year and we'll water up these horses and fill our canteens one last time with this stinkin' bad water before we make the crossin'. And once we get to Reno, as they're startin' to call 'er, we'll almost be to the Comstock Lode."

Twice, even with all of Joe's experience, they had gotten bogged down in quicksand, and once they'd had to rope and pull the black mare out or she would have floundered and sunk. As a result, the Paiute pony was hurt and lamed, so they set her free to forage along the grassy bed of the river. Paiutes or pilgrims would capture her sooner or later. Since that time, they had been riding the strawberry roan double, or else Fiona was walking because Joe's feet still weren't completely healed.

Now they were almost to the end of the Humboldt, and suddenly, Fiona was afraid again. They had not hooked up with any wagon trains, and Fiona was thinking about how they would soon be in Reno among other women.

"Joe," she said, "I know you want me to stay in Reno, but I just don't think I can do that when you ride up to Virginia City."

"It'd sure be for the best," Joe said. "I'm gonna have to face Peabody and either have a meeting of the minds or else kill him. After that, I figure to grab Jessica out of that

Catholic church and then come back down to Reno to get you. It could all happen sorta sudden, Fiona. It might not work as good if you come up to the Comstock Lode with me. After all, you're wanted for murder in Virginia City and your face is better known up there than mine."

"I know. I know!" Fiona took a deep breath and expelled it in frustration. "But what if things go wrong for you in Virginia City? What if . . . God forbid . . . Mr. Peabody and his men kill or arrest you?"

"I won't let that happen," Joe said stubbornly.

"But it *could* happen! And there I'd be, sitting and worried sick down in Reno and you up there in jail . . . or worse . . . and I wouldn't be able to help you at all."

Joe nodded with understanding because everything that his wife was saying was true. Bad things could happen to him. He might very well be shot to death . . . or, even worse, arrested and hanged.

"The thing of it is, Fiona. If I fail up there, then you're still safe in Reno and you could still figure out some way to get our daughter back. So you see, if you and I don't go up on the Comstock Lode together, it's like we'll have *two* chances to get Jessica instead of just one."

"All right, Joe. I trust your judgment, but I'm awfully worried."

"You have every right to be," he told her. "Now let's get moving. I'd like to hit that long stretch of deep sand about sundown so we can make our crossing in the night and most of tomorrow. If all goes well, we'll be in Reno tomorrow night and we can wash the salt and alkali away until we cross this damn desert again with our daughter."

"All right, Joe."

Joe reached down from the strawberry and held his wife's sunburned face in his rough hands. "Forty miles of heartache next, then another twenty miles to our daughter. That's all we have yet to go."

"So near and yet she seems so very far. Do you think Jessica will still remember me, Joe?"

"Of course!"

"She hasn't seen me in months now and she's only four years old."

"She'll remember her own mother," Joe promised. "She won't know me 'cause I only got to see her for a minute or two, but we'll have years to get to know each other after we put all this bloody Comstock bounty business behind us."

"I know. I know."

"Well," Ransom Holt said, his anger at the boiling point. "We got the damned buckboard stuck in quicksand and we lost a day's time. Then Paiutes stole my four good Missouri mules and all we've got are our horses and weapons. I hate this desert and, by damned, I'll never cross it again!"

"That's for sure," Redman said, knowing that the big man would miss the point he was making.

"My guts have been growling for a week and I've had the shits from all this bad water."

"It cleans a man out," Redman agreed. "But we're plenty lucky to be alive, given the Paiutes that snuck into our camp and took those mules. And we'd better make some good time today or we'll never even catch up with Joe Moss and his wife before they reach the Comstock Lode."

"Dammit!" Holt's big face was bright red and peeling. His lips were cracked and bloody from the sun and the hot wind and he had lost at least fifty pounds in this crossing. "You think that I don't know that? You're the damned Indian. How far ahead of us is Joe and Fiona, judging from these tracks?"

"Less than five miles now."

"Then let's go!"

Ransom Holt whipped his skinny, faltering horse into a gallop, but Johnny Redman followed at an easy, sensible trot. Their mounts had been considerably weakened by the desert crossing and, like the men that rode them, had been afflicted with diarrhea. They were terribly thin and without strength, and Holt ought to have realized that running their poor horses before that stretch of deep sand ahead was a foolish, foolish thing to do. If he killed his horse, then Holt would have to walk across forty miles of deep, waterless sand and Redman doubted that the white man could make it.

Fiona and Joe left the dying Humboldt River and forged into the deep sand. Despite Fiona's protests, Joe insisted on walking while his wife rode and led their burro into the deadly Humboldt Sink. Darkness fell and the air became cooler. The river sank into the sand, and soon after that they began to see the reminders of past heartaches that Joe had foretold. Entire wagons abandoned, skeletons of mules, horses, dogs, and even cattle that had come so far and then had died of thirst and exhaustion.

Coyotes howled in the darkness, gnawing on the freshest bones, and Fiona saw sun-cracked pianos and furniture that had probably once been some pioneer woman's pride and joy. She even saw a once-beautiful harp, probably a family heirloom from Ireland, and realized how devastating it must have been to throw it off a wagon like a piece of firewood.

"Oh," she said to Joe as they struggled through the deep sand, passing three crude crosses tilted by wind, eerie and luminous in the half moonlight, "this is a heartbreaking, killing place!"

"It might be a good idea just to keep your eyes straight ahead," Joe told her. "A lot of bad things to see here. That's another reason why I wanted to take you through it at night-time."

Fiona clutched her lead rope to the burro and the leather reins. She could feel the strawberry roan sink and struggle with each step, and she felt bad for the animal. Behind her, the little burro sometimes had to buck as if through water when the sand was deepest; both of the animals were gasping with their supreme effort.

Forty miles of hell.

Up until now, Fiona had thought that crossing below the Great Salt Lake had been terrible with its blowing salt and alkali dust . . . but this crossing was nightmarish and a hundred times worse. No, a *thousand* times worse. At least out on the great salt flats there had been nothing. But this . . . this was a hideous graveyard of death, shattered hopes, and destroyed dreams.

All through the night, she kept asking Joe how he was doing and feeling. She wanted to know if his feet were starting to bleed again.

"I got 'em wrapped in soft blanket wool," he said. "This sand is real soft so I'm doin' fine. Don't worry so much about me. Just keep looking ahead and keep those animals movin'."

"I will. I will."

Dawn finally came, and with it the full enormity of the devastation and heartache that surrounded them. Fiona saw miles and miles of bleached bones, grave markers, furniture, wagons, and tools. Some of the abandoned wagons had sunk up to their axles, and showed signs that incredible efforts had been made to free them from the deep, clutching sand . . . all to no avail. There were bone-white sand dunes, some of them already wind-whipped over the wagons to bury them forever, leaving no bad memories in sight.

But now, after a night of desperate slogging through this white hell, Fiona clearly saw the mountains—the high, blue green Sierras—and that gave her a surge of real, heart-thumping hope. Reno was near. The big, swift, and clear Truckee River was just up ahead, and there they could swim and laugh and even rest for a few precious days.

Yes, those mountains were growing bigger and bolder with every struggling hour and they were almost . . . almost there!

Joe was staggering, but his chin was lifted, and being a mountain man, his eyes were fixed on the highest peaks.

"We've made it, darlin'. We've made it!"

"Do we have to come back through this terrible Humboldt Sink?"

He stopped, feet buried a foot deep in sand. "No," he said as much to himself as to his wife. "We don't. When we leave the Comstock with Jessica, we can go northwest. Up into Oregon and then over and across through the Blackfoot country and into the wild Tetons. Thataway, we'd just miss the deserts altogether, Fiona."

As he spoke, the excitement grew in his gravelly voice. "If we went to the Tetons or the Big Horns, I got friends among the Indians and maybe some old mountain men still. Good friends that remember me as Man Killer. They'd take us in . . . or give us some land to live on for free."

"Is it pretty, Joe? Are those mountains where your friends can be found as pretty as the ones I see up ahead?"

"Yes, ma'am," Joe said with a painful grin. "They are real, real pretty! Not as pretty as you . . . but pretty all the same."

"Oh, Joe, you are such a sweet-talkin' man!"

He laughed. Laughed for the first time since the night they'd made love in the Ruby Mountains. "I'll sure give you more o' that when we get finished in these parts. I'll sweet-talk you and our little girl till your cheeks shine red as apples."

Fiona's chin lifted, too. "We'll have a *good* life together at last."

"We will and so will all our children. I was always happiest in the high mountains, Fiona. Never happy in flat land or in these deserts. So that's what we'll do, by golly! We'll not cross this godforsaken desert again, but instead go north up through California. You ever seen the Pacific Ocean?"

"No."

"Well, maybe I'll just take you by there for a look-see. You and Jessica. Maybe that's what I should do so's you kin both see it before we head back to the Tetons and the Big Horns. 'Cause once we get to those places, you'll never want to go anywhere ever again, girl o' mine."

"I can hardly wait!" she cried, almost weeping at the thought of such joyfulness after the long passage through a world of such death and heartache.

"Then, by jiminy, that's exactly what we'll do!" Joe shouted to the mountains as he marched through the last of the deep, clinging sands.

✢ 24 ✢

JOE MOSS DROPPED as a big-caliber rifle boomed and its bullet punched into sand near his feet. He whirled around to see Ransom Holt and Johnny Redman closing in on them fast. Joe raised his Spencer rifle, and was about to fire when the two onrushing horsemen split apart in order to set up a deadly cross fire.

Joe shot Ransom Holt's flagging horse and the animal cartwheeled, pitching the big man over its head into a sand dune. The half-breed changed directions, taking his horse out of Joe's rifle range. Redman made a flying dismount and with rifle in hand, dove behind a sand dune. Joe sent a shot in Redman's direction, knowing he was wasting a bullet, but wanting the man to understand he was a target.

"Fiona!" Joe shouted. "Get on that strawberry and ride like the wind for Reno! I'll stay here and hold them off!"

"I won't leave you!"

The half-breed fired and Joe could almost feel the .50-caliber slug whipcrack across the hot desert air and miss him by inches. "Fiona, do it before he shoots the horse and we're both afoot and helpless out here! I can hold them off until you bring me help!"

Joe knew that there wasn't going to be any help this far from Reno. But he wanted his wife out of rifle range and on her way to safety. "Go!"

Fiona jumped back into the saddle and with their little pack burro still tethered to her saddle horn, she sent the horse and burro into a run through the last few miles of sand dunes.

Ransom Holt had picked himself up from his bad fall and quickly taken cover behind a low sand dune. "Moss," the giant shouted, "if you want your wife to live, you'd better surrender now!"

Joe considered the angry demand. He was trapped. If he tried to get up and run away, the half-breed with his big rifle would shoot to wound, probably in the legs, because Joe was worth more to Peabody alive than dead. And if Joe tried to hunker down and fight, he would soon be delirious from lack of water. And his Spencer was no match for the much more powerful buffalo rifle.

"Moss, you hear me?" Holt shouted again. "Give up or we'll kill you right here and now!"

"What about the bounty money?" Joe yelled. "Peabody wants me alive!"

"We don't always get what we want, and he'll pay us handsomely for your head! You're pinned down and you're finished. The best you can do is to try and stay alive long enough to see your woman once more before you hang."

Joe considered his almost nonexistent options carefully. He had no canteen. He was outgunned and outnumbered. Even worse, he was trapped in a low, sandy place and there was nowhere to hide. And if all that wasn't desperate enough, the half-breed was finishing reloading the buffalo rifle and was about to kill him or perhaps even Fiona, who was still within his shooting range because of the slow-moving burro.

Maybe, Joe reasoned, after he surrendered and before they could get him tied hand and foot, he could somehow figure a way to kill both men. That wasn't likely, but it was his best and only choice of action.

"All right!" Joe finally shouted. "Just let my wife go free!"

Ransom Holt's laugh was cracked and cruel. "You're in no position to bargain, Moss. Throw that rifle out along with your pistol and that tomahawk you're so famous for using to scalp men."

"I gave my 'hawk to Paiutes clear back by the Ruby Mountains!"

"Then throw away your weapons and stand up with your hands in the air!"

When Joe did as he was told, the half-breed lowered his rifle a hair, and Joe looked at Fiona, trying to make her horse and the poor burro lunge through the deep, clinging sand.

"I'll take care of Moss," Ransom said. "Breed, you catch the Moss woman and bring her back here alive."

Johnny Redman nodded. "She'll be easy enough to overtake and the bounty on her head is as big as the one on Man Killer's head."

"Bigger. She's the one that murdered Chester Peabody. Now quit jawin' and run her down!"

The half-breed jumped on his horse, which Joe could see still had some run left in its legs. There wasn't any doubt that Johnny Redman would quickly overtake Fiona.

Holt cocked back the hammer of his Colt and aimed it at Joe's chest. "All right, Moss. Keep your hands up in the air and walk straight toward me."

Joe knew that the man would not hesitate to kill him if

he made the slightest wrong move. "You got me cold," he said. "Just go easy on that trigger."

"That's close enough," Holt said when Joe was less than ten feet from him. "Did you really think that we'd give up the chase?"

"Nope," Joe said. "I always knew that sooner or later it would come down to this. To just you and me."

Holt's face was red, wet with perspiration, and plastered with sand where it had struck the dunes when his horse was shot. "If you weren't worth so much more to Peabody alive than dead, I'd blow a hole in you right now. I'd gut-shoot you so you'd flop down in this sand and die screaming. And maybe I would even scalp you before your last breath so you could taste a little of your own Injun medicine."

Joe said nothing, but his mind was exploring every possible way he could kill this man before being tied hand and foot and taken to be hanged on the Comstock Lode.

"I never thought it would take so long to earn the bounty put on your head, Joe. I have to hand it to you . . . you're tougher than a boot and a hell of a lot smarter than you look."

"Johnny Redman better not hurt my wife," Joe said, turning to look to the west, where his wife and the half-breed had vanished.

"Ah, he won't. The breed is smart and he's desperate for his share of the bounty. He'll do what I ordered and he'll capture Fiona, but he won't hurt her unless he has to. He knows that Peabody wants your wife alive and healthy."

Joe almost smiled when he heard that the half-breed wasn't really the cold-blooded killer he made himself out to be. "So, Ransom, what do we do now?"

Holt glanced sideways at his dead horse. "You shot my horse through the heart on the run. Damn good shooting,

Moss. I might as well cut the reins from his bit and use them to tie your wrists and ankles."

"Yeah, I guess you just might as well. Oh, I was aiming at you, Holt, not the horse."

The giant laughed, and it had a mean, nasty sound. "Maybe you're not the crack shot I thought you were."

"We all make mistakes," Joe said with a shrug of his broad shoulders.

Holt extracted a pocketknife from his pants, and he shifted the Colt revolver into his left hand while he used his right to slice the reins away from the bit rings. Everything seemed to stand still except the wind, which was moaning across the lonely sand dunes. Joe watched and waited for just the right instant to attack. He knew that Holt was right-handed, but now the pistol was in the giant's left hand while he folded the pocketknife against his pants and started to return it to his pocket.

"There," Holt said, the blade clicking shut. "These are good rawhide braided reins. You won't break them. Turn around and put your hands behind your back. No foolishness or I'll shoot you in the spine. It might be more interesting to see a half-paralyzed man swing from the gallows. Bring a tear to the lady's eyes, I'll bet, while all the time I'd be laughing and counting my bounty money."

Joe moved toward the big man and started to lower his hands so that they could be tied. He understood that, once bound, he was helpless, so he'd made the decision to attack.

For a moment the two tall men stood face-to-face, and then Holt unexpectedly backhanded Joe with his Colt Army. The front sight on the barrel ripped through flesh all the way down to Joe's cheekbone and opened a wide and bloody gash.

Joe staggered and took a deep breath to instantly clear his mind again.

"Turn around, Moss, or I'll—"

Joe slashed downward with his right fist and knocked the Colt Army aside even as a bullet exploded into the sand. Then Joe threw his shoulder into Holt's broad chest with all the power he had left in his weary legs. They both crashed into the sand, rolling and fighting.

Holt was bigger and stronger, but Joe was the more experienced Indian wrestler and he knew that, no matter what, he could not allow the giant to get on top of him. When that seemed likely, Joe jammed a thumb deep into Holt's eyeball and twisted it sideways. The giant screamed and punched Joe so hard in the side of the head that he nearly blacked out.

Holt dove at Joe with bended knees to crush him, but Joe grabbed a handful of sand and threw it into the giant's one remaining good eye, blinding him.

Joe bit hard into Holt's left thumb. The Colt fell to the sand, and Joe scooped it up and sent three shots into Holt's wide-open mouth, blowing brains and blood out of his skull. Ransom Holt was finally dead.

Joe lay beside the giant, gasping for air and staring up at the merciless sun while catching his breath and waiting for his poor head to stop spinning.

Fiona!

Joe pushed himself to his feet and stared toward Reno and the direction his wife had gone with the half-breed closing on her back trail.

"Fiona!" he bellowed into the moaning wind.

For all the answer he got, Joe might as well have been standing on the surface of the moon. Still dazed and bleeding from the nasty gash across his cheekbone, Joe had never felt so desperate and helpless. How far had Fiona gotten before the half-breed had overtaken her? A mile? Maybe even two. Probably much less.

If she had been willing to release their burro, maybe, just maybe, she could have made it on the strawberry to Reno. But Joe knew his wife loved their little burro and she would not let it go until it was too late.

Joe snatched up Holt's weapons and emptied the man's pockets, taking cash without bothering to spend the time counting it. He then allowed himself one final look at the giant bounty hunter who had dogged him and his poor wife for so long. Holt's one good eye was staring up at the hot sun; the other eye, which Joe had gouged half out with his thumb, protruded ghoulishly like a purple grape that had been stomped in a pool of already congealing blood.

Joe *had* to find Fiona.

Had to save her from the half-breed before it was too late. But they were on horseback and he was on two mending feet, so right now things were not the least bit in his favor.

✢ 25 ✢

JOHNNY REDMAN HAD overtaken Fiona Moss, but it had required almost two hard miles of riding through the sand. Now, with his six-gun in his hand and riding stirrup to stirrup with the woman, Johnny shouted, "Rein up or I'll shoot the burro first, your horse second, and you last!"

Fiona glanced sideways at the tall young man through her tears. "No, let us alone!"

Johnny cocked back the hammer of his gun, aimed it at the baying and struggling little burro, and fired. He intentionally put a round hole through the tip of the burro's long, droopy ear. The burro bawled in pain; Fiona let out a scream and pulled the strawberry roan to a stop.

"You killed him! You killed that poor little—"

"I didn't kill him," Johnny said. "If I had wanted to kill him, I could have with both my eyes shut tight. He's just got a little hole in the tip of his ear, that's all."

Fiona scrubbed the tears from her eyes. "What is wrong with you? Why would you want to see Joe and me hang?"

"For the bounty," the half-breed said without anger. "I got to have the money."

"Do you need it bad enough to have our souls weighing on your conscience the rest of your life?"

"I'm afraid that I do." Redman reached out and took the reins from Fiona's hand. "We're going back now. Are you armed?"

"I have a gun."

"Give it to me."

Joe had given her the Colt Navy, and the thought passed through Fiona's mind that she could draw it out of her saddlebag and try to shoot Johnny Redman. But then she looked at the gun in his hand and saw that she wouldn't stand a chance.

"All right."

"It's loaded?"

"Yes."

"Then why didn't you try to kill me?" he asked, taking the gun from her hand.

"I thought about it."

"Just thinking never got anything done," Johnny told her. "I believe that you didn't try to use it because you can't kill anyone."

Anger flushed her cheeks. "I could kill Ransom Holt! And I could have killed those men at the dugout that did me wrong. I thought every living moment about how good it would feel to kill those three."

"Maybe," Johnny said. "But I doubt it. Don't matter. Your husband has done enough killing for both your lifetimes."

"For what it's worth," Fiona told him, "I didn't kill that rich man in Virginia City."

"I doubt that you did," Johnny answered. "But that

doesn't change the fact that there's a big bounty on your head for me to collect. Now let's head on back as fast as we can. By now, Ransom Holt has your man hog-tied and if we don't come back quick, he just might do something real, real bad to Joe Moss. You see, Ransom is just that kind of a man."

"And you're not?" she challenged.

"No time for—"

They both heard the three shots in quick succession.

"Oh, my God!" Fiona cried. "He did kill my poor husband!"

"Let's go!" Johnny ordered. "Leave the burro. We'll come back for him later!"

Fiona put her heels to her poor, worn-out strawberry roan. Johnny Redman was riding a fine pinto, and they raced side by side back across the shifting sand dunes.

"Look!" Fiona cried. "Why, that's my Joe! He . . . he must have *killed* Ransom Holt!"

Johnny did something totally unexpected. He reached out and shoved Fiona from her saddle. Had she landed on hard ground or rocks, she would have been badly injured, but she landed in the deep sand. Johnny grabbed the strawberry's reins and brought both horses to a stop. Then he turned them around and went back to Fiona, who was dazed and just coming to her feet.

Dismounting and grabbing Fiona, Johnny said, "Let's walk back side by side to meet him."

"But—"

"Do as I tell you," Johnny ordered, leading both horses. "Because if you don't, I'll kill Joe and then I'll kill you."

Fiona understood and nodded in agreement.

When they reached Joe, Johnny said, "You're armed and I'm armed, but my gun is pointed at your wife."

"If you—"

"Drop your gun, Joe," the half-breed ordered. "Drop it right now or I'll kill your wife."

"Don't do it!" Fiona cried. "He's just going to take us to hang! Shoot him, Joe!"

Joe had three bullets left in his revolver, but Johnny would have six. Joe was a fair-to-middlin' shot with a pistol; Johnny was the best and fastest man he had ever seen with a six-gun. And finally, Johnny had Fiona right next to him and he couldn't miss her even if he tried.

"All right," Joe said, the bile rising in his throat so that it nearly choked him.

"No!" Fiona cried. "Don't you see, he'll just take us to Peabody the same as Ransom Holt was going to do?"

"Yeah," Joe said bitterly, dropping the gun at his side. "But Ransom is dead and now we only got to do what this one tells us to do."

"I don't want to kill either of you," Johnny told them. "But I need the bounty money."

"For what!" Fiona cried. "To—"

"My people are up near the Big Horns and last winter twenty-six of them starved to death because the crooked reservation agent pocketed the government money that should have gone for provisions," Johnny said. "This winter, even more will die unless I can do something to save them."

Joe squinted. "Something like kill us for the Virginia City ransom?"

"Something like," Johnny admitted. "With a couple of thousand dollars I can buy cattle. Enough cattle and land to start a ranch up there next to our reservation. And my herds will grow and I'll feed my people every winter until the white agent is either dead or fired. I'll feed my people until a white man's justice finally comes to our reservation."

"Maybe I could kill that rotten Indian agent for you and that would take care of the problem," Joe suggested.

"If you or I did, someone just like him would take his place. Someone just like him *always* ends up in charge! But if I buy land and cattle, no one can take them away. I will *own* the land. I will *own* the cattle. They will be mine to give freely!"

"Taking us to Virginia City is wrong," Joe said. "No good comes from bad."

"It will this time," Johnny countered. "It is my only choice. Your lives . . . or the lives of many of my people this winter."

Joe looked at Fiona and his shoulders slumped. "I think we'd better do as this breed says for now, darlin'."

She scrubbed at her tears. "We were so close, Joe. So close to getting our daughter back and then going—"

"Shhh," he told her, not wanting his wife to let this half-breed know where they had decided to settle in peace for the rest of their days.

Fiona understood.

"You got any other guns on you, Joe?"

"No."

"No tomahawk and no knife?"

Joe threw his knife into the sand. "That's all."

The half-breed picked up the knife. "How did you kill Ransom Holt?"

"Why do you care?"

"I'd like to know."

"I shot him in the face three times with his own pistol. He was stronger, but I was quicker and I know how to Indian wrestle."

"Did you scalp him?"

"No time . . . and besides," Joe added, "I promised my wife that my scalpin' days were over."

"Man Killer will scalp no more?"

"That's right."

Johnny Redman picked up Joe's gun and blew the sand from it before he shoved the revolver behind his cartridge belt. Sounding sad, he pointed his gun at Joe and said, "Let's turn back west and we'll pick up that ear-shot burro on our way to Virginia City."

"How about you let my wife ride her horse."

"Maybe later," Johnny said. "For now, we'll all go for a little walk."

Joe turned and then said back over his shoulder, "We can start out, but we ain't walking far. Those are Paiutes and they got our pack burro."

Johnny Redman glanced over his shoulder, expecting the worst and seeing it. "We're surrounded by them."

Joe turned a full circle. "Must be at least fifty. So, Johnny, you're the man with the gun in his hand. What are you gonna tell us to do now?"

For once, the half-breed had no words, no thoughts. He could try to make a run for it alone, but he knew he stood no chance and they would overtake and kill him.

"I guess we see if we can make a deal," Johnny finally answered.

"What kind of a deal?" Joe asked. "Do you think these people are gonna take me and Fiona to the Comstock Lode for that blood bounty?"

"No," Johnny said. "I don't."

"And do you think they'll settle for keepin' our burro?"

"I very much doubt it."

"Maybe," Joe said, "you'd better give me back a gun and then at least we can put up some kind of a fight."

"I'm considering it," the half-breed told him. "I'm strongly considering it."

"Well, consider fast," Joe said, "because here they come!"

✢ 26 ✢

"ALL RIGHT," JOHNNY Redman said, handing Joe a loaded pistol as the Paiutes jumped off their ponies and started forward with guns and rifles. "I guess we might as well go down giving them a good fight."

"Fiona needs a gun, too," Joe said. "After we kill some, they won't take kindly to a woman captive. They'll treat her real bad."

"Can she shoot straight?" Johnny asked.

"I can," Fiona said, watching the Paiutes drop to the sand and start crawling in on them from all sides.

"Save the last 'un for yourself," Joe told her. "Or I'll do it."

"I can do it," Fiona told him. "And remember this one thing, Joe."

He looked at his wife. Her face was cut and blistered from sand and sun, but Joe had never thought her more brave nor beautiful. "What?"

"I love you, Joe. Despite all the terrible things that have happened to us since we met, we created a beautiful daughter,

Jessica. And even if we never see her again, a part of us will live on."

Joe Moss wasn't an emotional man, but when he heard those words from Fiona, he nearly cried. Instead, he bit his lip until it bled and cocked back the hammer of his pistol.

"We wait until they're real close, and then we stay low in the sand and shoot fast and straight."

"Amen to that," the half-breed whispered, swiveling his body around so that he was facing away from where Joe and Fiona were facing.

Suddenly, Fiona cried, "Joe! We have that medicine man's stick! The one painted red with the eagle feather. He said it would give us protection!"

"Holy hog fat, you're right!" Joe crowed. "I'd completely forgotten about that powerful medicine stick."

"Joe, it's gotta work!"

"I don't know," he said, "but I damn sure mean to find out."

"I'm faster than you afoot," Redman said. "Exactly where is it!"

"In the saddlebag on the right side of the strawberry roan."

"Cover me!" Johnny hissed as he jumped up and ran to the strawberry roan.

The horse wasn't more than ten yards away, but when Johnny Redman made his swift move, the Paiutes opened fire. Johnny was creased in the leg and he staggered, but still lunged for the strawberry, which shied away from him.

"Easy. Easy," Johnny said as a hailstorm of bullets and arrows whizzed all around. The half-breed thrust his hand into the saddlebags and drew out the carved red medicine man's stick with its beautiful eagle feather.

Johnny spun around and another bullet sliced across his

ribs. He fell back against the strawberry, which bolted and ran off into the desert. Joe knew that he would never see that good horse again because the Paiutes would capture it as a prize that had once belonged to Man Killer.

"Hey! Hey-ya! Hey-ya! Hey!" Johnny shouted a Cheyenne chant as he spun a full circle waving the medicine man's stick.

The firing died. Johnny, balanced on one good leg and leaking blood from his ribs, kept chanting and waving the red medicine stick.

"It's working!" Fiona cried. "Look!"

"I kin see," Joe said, watching as the Paiutes all around them suddenly lowered their weapons and stood up watching the half-breed. After a moment, one of them gave a signal and all the Paiutes quietly started toward them as Johnny kept up his dancing and chanting in Cheyenne.

A short time later, those Paiutes were riding away. Their medicine man, a deep walnut-colored little fellow, had given Johnny Redman some salve for his wounds. In return, Johnny had offered the old medicine man his handsome pinto, which was received with great formality and happiness.

"How badly are you wounded?" Fiona asked, coming to Johnny's side.

"If I can lean on your shoulder, I think I can make it out of this desert to Reno. It'll be slow, but I can do 'er."

"I'll be slow, too, with these sorry damned feet o' mine," Joe said. "We're gonna be a damned sorry sight when we limp into Reno."

"Just as long as we make it," Johnny said.

Joe looked at the half-breed closely. "What about that bounty on our heads?"

"You and Fiona saved my life with that red Paiute medicine stick and eagle feather. My people believe that when someone saves your life, you can never take their life."

"That a fact?" Joe asked, making sure.

"It is," Johnny assured them.

"Hmmm," Joe mused. "Seems like the Blackfoot have that same rule . . . or maybe it's the Crow. I forget."

"Well, I'm Cheyenne," Johnny told them, "and that's the way that we believe."

"Then I guess I won't have to kill you either, Johnny Redman. What's your Cheyenne Indian name?"

"Stalking Wolf."

"I'm gonna call you Wolf from now until we part," Joe told the young half-breed. "You can call me either Joe or Man Killer."

Wolf nodded. "And what do I call your woman?"

"Call her brave," Joe said. "Now let's git outa this damned desert and settle the score in Virginia City."

Wolf said, "I might still collect the bounty."

"Oh?" Joe asked.

"But I will never do you or Fiona harm and I will never let you be harmed."

"In that case," Joe said, "you're a good wolf and we are friends."

The Paiutes had taken the strawberry roan, but they'd left the burro alone. When Joe, Fiona, and Wolf finally limped into Reno, they traded the faithful little burro for ammunition and a few meager supplies.

"Joe," Wolf asked, "tell me what you know about the Comstock Lode. Is it a bad place?"

"It's about as sinful as they get," Joe told the half-breed as they rode in a stagecoach up the winding and desolate mountain road leading to Virginia City.

"What is your plan?"

"Don't have one actually," Joe admitted.

"I should have guessed that much," Wolf said with a grin. "Maybe we should think of a plan before we get there."

"Yes, Joe. Wolf is right," Fiona said. "We ought to think of something."

"All right," Joe cheerfully agreed. "How about you two get Jessica and I go down to Peabody's Shamrock Mine and I kill him? After that, I'll join up with you two right here on the road back down to Reno."

"No!" Fiona argued. "You can't go face Peabody all alone!"

"Sure I can," Joe told them. "I can . . . and I will. This blood feud is between me and the last Peabody standing. We'll either make peace . . . or I'll suddenlike kill the rich sonofabitch."

"That's a very good plan," Wolf said as their stagecoach climbed the steep grade. "But I want the bounty and I'm going with you."

"It could get unhealthful."

"It could," Wolf agreed as he patted the six-gun on his lean hip, "but I'll take my chances with you."

"Fair enough," Joe told the half-breed.

"Joe," Fiona said. "Don't you think we ought to go to St. Mary's and see Jessica before . . . well, before you and Wolf go down to have it out with Peabody?"

"I would like to see that girl one last time . . . just in case things don't go well down at the Shamrock Mine. But it'd be easier on my mind to first have that showdown. That way, I'll only be thinkin' about killin' the man that sent bounty hunters off to get us hung."

"I'll get a room at the Gold Strike Hotel at this end of C Street. I won't leave my room until you come back for me and Jessica."

"See that you don't," Joe warned her. "There are people

here on the Comstock Lode who will remember you and make a try for that bounty money that's on your head."

Joe hailed the stagecoach driver, and the man pulled his team up at the hotel. Fiona hugged and kissed Joe good-bye, and then she also hugged Wolf, saying, "You two watch each other's backs."

"We will," Wolf promised. "If we could survive two run-ins with Paiutes and that desert crossing, we'll do all right against Peabody and his friends."

"I'll be waitin' and prayin' for both of you," Fiona said, hurrying into the hotel without a backward look because she didn't want them to see her tears.

"You two leavin' that little woman and goin' on into Virginia City?" the driver asked.

"We are," Joe said. "Actually, we're goin' over the Divide and down into Gold Hill."

"I'm drivin' this stage right on through Gold Hill. What business you fellas got there?" the man asked.

"We got a settlin' business to take care of."

"A what?"

"Never mind," Wolf said. "Just take us over the Divide and drop us off in front of the Shamrock Mine. We have business with Mr. Garrison Peabody."

"You fellas don't look like hard-rock miners to me. Besides, I don't believe that Peabody is hirin' right now."

"We've come a long, hard way," Joe growled. "Just quit the jawin' and drive us down to the Shamrock Mine."

"All right, but you don't have to get scratchy about it!" the driver growled.

Once Joe and Wolf were back in the stagecoach and all by themselves, Wolf said, "Are we just going to go in there and get the drop on Peabody and his bunch?"

"That's the general idea," Joe replied. "And then I'll ask the rich man real nice if he wants to step outside and settle this thing between us once and for all. Wolf, your job is to make sure that one of Peabody's men don't back-shoot me while I'm carvin' up their boss."

"I can do that," Wolf assured him.

The stagecoach made a short stop in Virginia City and took on a few passengers bound for Carson City. Joe and Wolf, faces cracked by wind and sun, bloodied, worn, and wounded by their desert trials, didn't even get a hello from the other passengers, who shrank as far away from them as possible.

"I guess maybe we should get a bath someday," Wolf said with a half smile. "These good city folks are acting like we're smellin' pretty ripe, Joe."

"Most likely because we are. But real soon, everything is about to change."

"Amen," Wolf replied, staring out the window at all the huge Comstock mines and wondering if he would even still be alive in one hour.

✢ 27 ✢

THE SHAMROCK MINE had been rebuilt after Joe Moss had blown it up with dynamite almost a year ago. Now the office was bigger, with clean windows and a large, impressive sign out in front. The hoisting works were all new, and the immense steam engines were thumping as they lowered and lifted men and ore from deep in the belly of Sun Mountain.

"It looks like they've rebuilt everything bigger and better since I blowed 'er all to smithereens," Joe observed as he and Wolf stepped down from the stagecoach and tipped the driver two bits for taking them over the Divide.

"The sign out front says that they're not hiring today," Wolf said, pointing.

"Yeah, I can read it," Joe said, checking the gun on his hip. "Are you ready?"

"Ready as I'll ever be," the half-breed told him.

"Then let's go in and get this bounty business settled once and for all."

Joe opened the door and stepped into the big mining

office. As he remembered from his last visit, there was a counter behind which were a roomful of desks and clerks at work, with a large private office in the back. On the door of the office were bold gold letters: GARRISON PEABODY, PRESIDENT.

A clerk wearing an eyeshade left his desk and approached the front counter. "If you men are looking for work, then you'll have to keep looking because we aren't hiring."

"I read that outside," Joe said, eyes fixed on Peabody's private office, whose interior was blocked from view by the closed door. "Is the big boss in that office right now?"

"If you mean Mr. Peabody, then yes."

"Good," Joe said, moving around the counter to a little swinging gate and pushing right through it on his way toward the private office.

"Wait a minute there!" the clerk shouted as everyone looked up from their paperwork. "You can't go in there without an appointment!"

"But we are," Wolf said, drawing his pistol and waving it at the roomful of staring clerks. "And I wouldn't advise anyone to try and stop us."

Joe was already at the door of the office, and he threw it open to see a large, clean-shaven gentleman in his forties dressed in a very expensive suit sitting behind an enormous oak desk. The man looked up and started to say something, but Joe spoke first.

"I'm Joe Moss, the man you sent Ransom Holt to bring back dead or alive along with my wife, Mrs. Fiona Moss."

Garrison Peabody's eyes grew wide with astonishment, and then he made a grab for a desk drawer, probably to reach a hideout pistol. But Joe was on him like a bird on a bug, and he kicked Peabody's swiveling desk chair into a full circle, and then he slapped the rich mine owner in his smooth, handsome face. The blow sounded like a shot, and Peabody was knocked out of his chair and against the wall.

"Stand up and let's finish this once and for all," Joe shouted. "Fists, guns, or knives. It's your choice, but make up your mind fast."

Peabody picked himself up and wiped his face. "You," he hissed, eyes filled with hatred.

Wolf drew his six-gun and pointed it out at the outer office so that there would be no unwanted interference.

"What's it gonna be?" Joe demanded, raising his fists. "A beating or a killin'? Either way is fine with me so long as we put our feud to rest."

Peabody rose to his full height and clenched his fists. Wolf had to give it to the rich mine owner; he wasn't some pampered coward frantically pleading for help from his employees.

Peabody lunged forward, swinging a hard right hand that, had it connected, would have sent Joe Moss staggering back into the large office. But Joe ducked and drove his own right hand into the rich man's gut, which proved soft. Peabody's mouth flew open and he gasped. Joe reared back and pounded a right cross that connected with Peabody's jaw, sending the rich man crashing to the floor.

"Get up!" Joe ordered. "You caused me and my wife more hardship and pain than I'll ever be able to put on you, but right now it's time for starters."

Peabody struggled to his feet, leaning heavily on the desk. His face had turned pale and his eyes were glassy.

"Get your fists up, rich man! I'm gonna beat you bloody and then I'm gonna cut your damned throat!"

Wolf turned back into the office and jammed the barrel of his gun into Joe's spine. "No, you're not," he said quietly.

"Because, Joe, if you as much as move, I'm going to kill you."

Joe stiffened and swallowed hard. "You sneaky half-breed sonofabitch! You tricked me!"

"That's right," Wolf said. "How else was I going to get you here so that I could collect that bounty money?"

"You're gonna fry in Hell!" Joe raged, feeling the barrel of Wolf's gun hard against his backbone. "I swear you will."

Peabody stepped forward and drove his meaty fist into Joe's gut, doubling him up. "So how does it feel, Moss?"

Joe started to lunge at the mine owner, but Wolf rammed his gun barrel into Joe's ear, saying, "Don't do it or I'll blow your mangy head clean off!"

Peabody hit Joe Moss again, this time in the face, and dropped him to the polished office floor.

"Ouch," Peabody said, rubbing his knuckles. "That hurt!"

"I brought him to you," Wolf said, glancing at a big safe in the corner of Peabody's office. "And I believe the bounty you were going to pay Ransom Holt was seven thousand dollars."

"That was for Moss *and* his wife," Peabody countered.

"Fiona Moss can be found at the Gold Strike Hotel on C Street. She's waiting for us to come back."

Joe spat blood at the polished office floor and cursed. "I don't know how, Wolf, but I'm gonna kill you!"

"Shut up!" Wolf shouted, eyes fixed on Garrison Peabody. "So I'll take that seven thousand dollars in cash right now."

"I . . . I don't have it all."

"Sure you do," Wolf said. "Open that big safe."

"There's not quite seven thousand in it. Maybe only a little over five thousand."

"I'll take that, and the rest when we put Fiona Moss's head in the noose."

Peabody smiled. "Well done! Just a moment and I'll get the safe open for you."

"I've been waiting a long time for that bounty money," Wolf admitted. "I reckon that I can wait another minute longer."

Garrison Peabody went to his safe and, concealing its combination lock from view with his thick body, he spun the dial and soon had the safe open. Wolf saw the man scooping out wads of cash and stuffing them into a canvas bank deposit bag. With his gun still trained on Joe, Wolf went to stand near the Shamrock Mine owner. "All of it, Mr. Peabody. Those gold and silver coins, too."

"Then this will be close to the seven thousand," Peabody was saying as he worked fast. "And by the way, what happened to Ransom Holt?"

"Joe Moss shot the back of his head off. He also killed Jedediah Charles and Ike. Joe Moss killed every man you sent . . . but you never sent me, and that's why I'm the one collecting the bounty."

"I don't care who collects, as long as I have them both ready to be hanged," Peabody said, standing up and handing the heavy canvas bag filled with coin and cash to Wolf. He reached into his office desk and drew out a gun. "Now that you've been paid, you can leave. I'll take care of Mr. Moss and his wife."

Quicker than the strike of a snake, Wolf slammed the barrel of his six-gun across the rich mine owner's face, knocking him unconscious to the floor.

"Get up, Man Killer," Wolf ordered. "We've been paid and we're ready to leave now."

Joe came to his feet, a look of disbelief on his face. "You mean you was just *actin'*?"

"That's right," Wolf confessed. "I didn't see any other way to get the bounty except to pretend that I was collecting it on you."

"Damn," Joe said, rubbing his jaw and looking from Wolf to Peabody and back to Wolf again. "You sure had me fooled!"

"It had to be that way," Wolf said, turning his gun toward the office. "All you people out there just stay seated and don't do anything stupid!"

Peabody moaned, and Joe turned back to the man. "I can't leave this unfinished."

"Joe," Wolf said, "he's whipped and I can't let you murder him. If I do that, then I'll be wanted for murder along with you. That's not the way that this is going to end."

"It'll end the way I say it'll end!" Joe shouted.

"I need this money for my people and you need some of it for your wife and child. Now let's go!"

Joe Moss had his hand on his holstered Colt revolver, and he wanted in the most terrible way to pull the gun out and shoot Garrison Peabody, but the man was on the floor and only half conscious.

"All right," Joe finally decided. He pointed a shaking finger at Peabody and said, "I killed two of your brothers, so I guess I can understand why you hate me so much. But Fiona never killed the first 'un and I won't have you comin' after us with more bounty hunters. You do, I'll come back and skin you alive! Hear me?"

Peabody managed to weakly nod his head.

"Good!" Joe exclaimed. "Wolf, let's get the hell outa here!"

Wolf thought that was a fine idea. He clutched a fortune in one hand and a gun in the other, and the future suddenly looked a whole lot better for his starving Cheyenne people.

They hurried outside and started up the road through

Gold Hill, holstering their guns and moving as fast as they could on foot. They crossed the Divide and then limped through Virginia City until they arrived at the Gold Strike Hotel. Fiona ran out the door and threw her arms around her husband, crying with happiness. Then she gave Wolf a hug for good measure.

"I'm going to find a livery and buy us three fast horses," Wolf told them. He hoisted the heavy bag filled with cash and coin. "I can buy the best now."

"Meet us down at St. Mary's where we'll be gettin' our little girl," Joe told the half-breed.

"I'll do it!"

Joe and Fiona ran all the way down the mountainside to burst breathlessly into the white-steepled Catholic church.

"Father O'Connor!"

The old Irish priest appeared holding hands with Jessica. "I saw you both running down here from C Street and I knew you'd finally come for this sweet and beautiful child of God."

"Jessica!" Fiona cried, throwing her arms around the girl. "We've come to take you with us this time."

Joe had a hard time keeping his emotions under control. Father O'Connor pulled him aside and said, "I have something to confess, Mr. Moss."

"You have something to confess to *me*?"

The priest nodded. "There was a man named Thurston Poole, a hard-drinkin' man who sometimes came to our church for Confession and absolution."

Joe was confused. "I never heard of Thurston Poole. What's he got to do with anything?"

"He was the one that stabbed Chester Peabody to death that bloody night in front of your wife's shack. Mr. Poole couldn't live with the guilt and he confessed the murder to me."

Fiona was holding their daughter, but she'd overheard the priest and now she stood to face him. "So . . . so you know that I didn't kill that man, Father?"

"I know," the priest answered quietly. "And Thurston Poole got so drunk and sick with guilt, despite his confession, that he shot himself in the head two weeks ago." Father O'Connor bowed his head and made the sign of the cross. "We had a Mass for his poor, tortured soul and we buried him up in our little Catholic cemetery."

"Father, why in God's name didn't you tell Garrison Peabody that my wife is innocent of his brother's death?" Joe demanded. "I was just at the Shamrock Mine and he doesn't know the truth yet."

The priest looked very ashamed of himself. "I meant to tell Mr. Peabody someday. But . . . but I didn't know you were coming back so soon and I just . . . well, I just didn't . . . yet."

"But you will!" Fiona cried. "Father, you must!"

"You have my word that I will tell him this very day that you were not the one that murdered Chester Peabody that dark and terrible night."

Fiona drew in a deep breath and studied the downcast Irish priest a moment before saying, "We all make mistakes, Father. Even priests. You and the nuns have taken care of our dear little girl out of love and kindness, and so I forgive you."

The priest smiled and took her hand in his own. "Thank you, my dear. And God go with you and your family always."

Fiona looked at Joe. "I think we should leave with our daughter right now."

"Yes," Joe agreed. "And Father, don't you be waiting any longer to tell that rich man that my Fiona is innocent."

"I swear on my mother's grave I'll go tell Mr. Peabody today."

"All right," Joe said, satisfied that at last the blood feud had been put to rest.

Wolf was waiting in front of the Gold Strike Hotel with three fine saddle horses. "They cost me five times as much as they're worth," he complained. "Everything up here costs a fortune."

"You have a fortune now," Joe reminded the half-breed.

Wolf handed Joe a small bag of cash. "It's not half, but it's still a lot of money, Joe. It'll buy you, Fiona, and that beautiful daughter a good start somewhere."

Joe was pleased. "Wolf, I'm taking my wife and daughter to see the Pacific Ocean before we go on to the high country."

"I've never seen an ocean," Wolf said, eyes on the Sierras. "Mind if I join you?"

"Nope," Joe said. "In fact, you can come with us all the way to the high country."

"And which high country would that be?" Wolf asked.

"The Big Horns," Joe told him.

"Why, that's my country, too!" Wolf said with a laugh.

Joe said to the half-breed, "So we're family now and we're going all the way together."

Stalking Wolf of the Cheyenne understood what was being said to him and he was glad. He had never really had a family, but now he and Joe Moss were brothers and would live out their days in peace in the big mountain country.

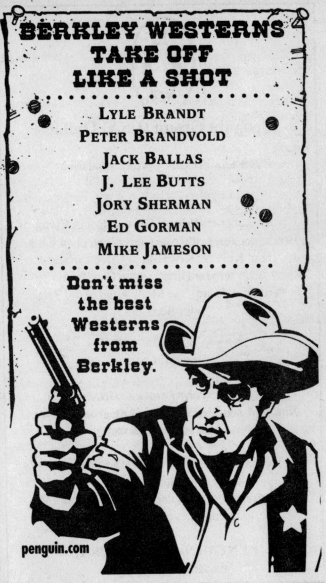